如何？

和老外打交道

≪ Basic English etiquette

≪ Recommendation

≪ Emotional expressions

基本英語禮儀、推薦、情緒表達法

How to Manage Special American Occasions

Preface

自　序

　　「世界日報」是北美最有名氣、銷售量最大的中文日報，我能在該報的「世界周刊」寫了十二年多的「實用英語」專欄，感到榮幸。

　　在那十二多年裡，前六年所發表的文稿，承蒙台灣大名鼎鼎的聯經出版公司為我出了三本書，其中一本也在大陸發行簡體版，我很開心。

　　本書是後六年中所發表一部分的集文，這次又蒙聯經出版，十分高興。

　　我在美四十多年，住過大小城市，曾在三所大學任職，接觸過不同階層的人士，深深了解美國人的生活禮節與人際關係。本書所談的情況，是咱們與老外交往中必須知道的部分。書中各種祝賀與安慰以及寫推薦信等等，也是老美平時使用的詞句，是道道地地簡潔明瞭的美語說法。讀者可從數百條的例句中，挑選合適的句子，需要時，可把主詞或動詞，稍加變更，即可集句成文。這種「偷懶」辦法，可節省華人許多時間和精力，合乎「實用」、「方便」的要求。

　　我講求實際，所以把英語生活化，因為世上沒有什麼事比生活更重要。

出書是許多教育者的心願，由於每個人的需求和看法不同，本書要想「人人稱好」可不容易。但我盡量做到內容充實，希望對讀者有所助益。

我不為「面子」問題而請求高官名人作序，不過我要感謝以下諸位：

聯經出版公司發行人林載爵先生對我文稿的興趣與採納。

北美世界書局總經理周才博先生對拙文的賞識和推薦。

專攻英美文學與寫作，深受本大學同仁敬佩的James Thrash教授，在我疑難時，作出指點。

「世界周刊」主編常誠容女士的審核，使拙文生色不少。

聯經出版公司主編李芃小姐的編審與協助，使本書趨於完善。

最後我感謝家人的鼓勵與支持。本書如能增進中美親友間的了解，是我最大的期盼。

我仍用筆名「懷中」，因為我沒有忘記自己是中華兒女，在做人處事上，我仍以「中庸之道」自勉。

懷中

Contents

目　錄

1. 每篇內容都有分類，每類舉例數十句，供人選用
2. 寫推薦信一文，內容五大類，舉例數百句，可以挑選組合
3. 是中、美人民生活交流的好信息

Time is money and this book saves your time.

Chapter *1*

老美生活禮節

　　美國人為了社會和諧，維持文明形象，特別重視生活禮貌，所以自小訓練，平時常說「謝謝」、「抱歉」、「不客氣」等等。（尤其在小城市）雖然帶有一些「做作」或「虛偽」，但讓人還有賞心悅目之感。老美認為生活禮貌，不但代表個人的品德修養和教育程度，也可顯示自己國家的美好形象。假如國民不懂生活禮節，即使國家富強，也難受到別人的尊重。

　　咱們老中如能了解老美的生活禮節，可以取人之長，補己之短，不但能增進中美人民間的友誼，也可提高老中的文明形象，我把老美的生活禮節，大致分為幾方面來說：

(1)說話禮節
(2)餐桌禮節
(3)公共場合的禮貌
(4)委婉或禮貌用語

 ## 說話禮節（Conversational manners）

　　一般老美與人說話，非常注意以下事項：

Always speak in a low voice; try to be a soft-spoken person.
說話聲音要低；做個說話聲音溫和的人。
或：Never talk over-loudly or in a high pitched voice.
說話嗓門不可太高或太尖銳。
(老美認為說話聲音大，就是不高興的表現)

Being a neat and well-groomed person is paying respect to others.

服飾整齊清潔，是尊敬他人的表現。

（well-groomed 指好好打扮，包括男子的梳頭和刮鬍）

Be sure to retain eye-contact with the person you are talking to.

與人說話時，眼睛要看著對方。

Let the other person talk about himself or herself first.

讓對方先說他／她自己的事。

Show your interest in other person's activity or accomplishment.

表現你愛聽別人的活動或成就。

Try to be patient as a good listener.

做個有耐心，愛聽對方說話的人。

A successful person does a lot of listening but very little talking.

一般成功的人，都是多聽少說。

Talk about what interests others, not about what interests you.

談些別人有趣的事，不要談你自己有趣的事。

Don't interrupt; to cut a person short in the middle of his/her conversation is unpardonable.

不可中途打斷別人的說話；那是不能原諒的。

Don't speak out before the speaker has given you permission to say something.

未得到演講者的許可前，不要說話。

Don't monopolize the conversation or talk about yourself continually.

不要滔滔不絕地談到自己，使別人沒有說話機會。

Don't brag too much about yourself or children's talents or academic success.

不要太吹噓自己，也不要太誇耀自己兒女的天分或學業的成就。

Never talk about other friend's shortcomings.

不可談到其他朋友的缺點。

Don't ask your friend's personal matters such as age, salary, expenditures, etc.

不要問朋友的私事，諸如年齡、薪水、開支情形等等。

Before you speak, ask yourself, "Is it true?" and "Is it kind?"

說話前，先問自己：「這是真的嗎？」「這是友善的嗎？」

Try not to talk about political or religious topics in gatherings.

朋友相聚時，不談政治或宗教事情。

Don't always make yourself the hero of your own stories.

不要老把自己說成「故事」中的英雄。

Don't be long-winded when you have something to say. Be direct, compact and right to the point.

說話不可嘮嘮叨叨，喋喋不休。要簡短，說出要點。

(long-winded 是形容詞＝talk too long)

For a good appearance while you are talking to someone, there should be no dandruff on your hair or shoulders.

為了好的外表，與別人說話，頭上和肩上不能有頭皮屑。

Don't be witty at another person's expense or ridicule anyone.

不要為了表現自己的聰明風趣而損害他人，也不要取笑任何人。

If you cannot say something nice, don't say anything at all.

如果你沒有什麼好話可說，那麼什麼都不要說。

Try not to repeat old jokes or tell time-worn stories.

不要重複老掉牙的笑話，或多次說過的故事。

(time-worn＝have been told over and over)

Don't talk about maladies or (about) your afflictions or other troubles.

不要談到自己的疾病、痛苦或其他的苦惱。

Try to avoid asking rude, presumptuous, inappropriate or embarrassing questions.

不要問些冒昧、不恰當或令人尷尬的問題。

Don't ask others about dyed hair, wigs, toupees or face-lifts.

不要問別人有關染髮；戴假髮或整容的事。

（wig 指女用假髮；toupee 是法文指男用假髮）

Watch out for bad breath; use some breath freshener before talking to others.

小心口臭；與別人談話前，先吃幾粒去口臭的糖片。

Don't try to improve someone except yourself.

不要想改進別人；改善自己就行。

When you converse with someone, don't come across as patronizing.

與別人談話時，不可有超越身分的表現。

（come across as patronizing＝appear as superior）

Don't break up the company by a sudden and premature departure.

不要突然或提早離開你的伙伴們。

For men, don't forget to pull up your zipper.(＝Don't let your fly be open.)

男人不可忘記拉上褲子的拉鍊。

Don't appear indifferent or impatient when others are talking.

別人說話時，不要顯得不在乎或不耐煩。

Listening politely to everyone is a cardinal necessity of good breeding.

有禮貌的留神細聽，是良好教養者所必要的。

Watch your mouth; restrain your urge to argue, criticize or complain.

小心說話；盡量控制你想爭論、批評或埋怨的衝動。

Don't be supercritical, heartless, mean or narcissistic.

不要過分吹毛求疵，狠心刻薄或自我陶醉。

(narcissistic 是孤芳自賞＝self-loving)

Don't chew your chewing gum while talking.

談話時，不要咀嚼口香糖。

Try to look as neat and good as you can; dress becomingly, talk softly and act courteously.

盡量讓自己看起來很整齊，穿得很恰當，說話很溫和，舉止很客氣。

餐桌禮節（Table manners）

老美與朋友吃飯時，也很重視以下的禮節。

Never talk with food in your mouth.

嘴裡有食物時，千萬不要張口說話。

Don't make noises as you are chewing.

吃東西時，不可發出聲音。

Take in small bites and chew quietly with your mouth closed. The worst thing is smacking of your food.

小口地吃，閉嘴輕輕地咬。吃東西出聲音，最不好。

（smacking＝making noises）

Don't make noises while eating soup or noodles.

喝湯吃麵時，不可發出聲音。

（喝湯叫 eat soup 或 have soup，但不叫 drink soup）

Don't let your eating behavior get under your friend's skin.

不要讓你朋友不高興你的吃飯行為。

（get under someone's skin＝upset someone）

Don't help others with their food; pass the dish and let them serve themselves.

不可幫別人夾菜；把菜傳過去，讓他們自己隨意拿。

Use the serving utensils; never use your own.

夾菜時，要用公用的匙或叉，不可使用自己用過的。

（這點，老美是特別注意）

Don't chew your food with your mouth open; it is rude and spoils others' appetite.

不要張開嘴巴咬東西；那是很不禮貌，破壞別人的食欲。

Don't stretch across another's plate to reach anything. Ask the person closest to the dish to pass it to you.

不要超越別人的碗盤去拿東西，請靠近菜餚的人為你傳送。

The way you conduct yourself at table is a reflection of your upbringing.

你在餐桌上的舉止，就能反映出你的教養。

Don't use your fingernail to pick the food particles from between the teech.

不可用指甲去挖牙縫裡的菜屑。

Never blow your nose at (the) table with your napkin.

千萬不要用餐巾擤鼻涕。

（table 前的 the 可省去）

Don't bend over your plate or drop your head to bring food to your mouth.

不要彎腰低頭把嘴對著碗盤吃東西。

（要用湯匙或叉子把食物送到嘴裡。）

Keep your elbows close to your side.

不要伸開你的胳膊；要保持在你的範圍。

（＝Don't spread out your elbows.）

Don't use a toothpick at (the) table; use it in the bathroom, instead.

不要在餐桌上用牙籤；到廁所去用。

Try not to hiccough at table while eating in company.

大家吃飯時，盡量不要打嗝。

（hiccough＝hiccup）

Don't pick your nose or ear while eating with friends.

和朋友吃飯時，不要挖鼻子或掏耳朵。

Never clear your throat in the presence of others at the table.

在餐桌上，不可在眾人面前清喉嚨。

Don't scratch your head at table while eating with others.

與別人吃飯時，不要抓頭。

（以免頭皮屑落到菜裡）

Never push someone to drink wine; it is always up to a person's desire.

不可勉強別人喝酒；一定要遵照別人的意願。

（老中千萬不要迫著老美乾杯）

If you ever happen to make gas during a meal with others, just ignore it.

與大家吃飯時，萬一不慎放屁，就裝著沒有這回事。

If you need to go to bathroom while eating, say, "Excuse me" without explaining the reason.

吃飯時，如要上廁，要說聲：「Excuse me.」，但不必解釋原因。

Use your spoon to bring soup to your mouth instead of holding the bowl to your mouth.

要用湯匙把湯送到嘴裡，不是把整個碗端到嘴裡喝。

Don't rise from the table until the meal is finished.

飯未吃完前，不要離開餐桌。

As a guest you should defer to the host / hostess.

客隨主便。

(defer to the host＝follow the host)

Don't try to outdress your hostess.

衣服不要穿得比女主人更華麗。

(outdress 是指 wear fancier clothes)

Certain food can be eaten with the fingers, such as chicken drumsticks and bread.

有些食物可用手指拿，諸如雞腿和麵包。

When you are invited for dinner or an outing, be punctual.

人家請你吃飯或外出，要守時。

Don't be the one holding up dinner.

不要做個耽擱吃飯的人。

If you have a loud voice in a restaurant, you'll attract the stares of many diners.

在餐館吃飯，如果說話聲音大，其他食客會盯著你看。

（美國餐館都是很安靜）

Bad table manners are a turn off for many people.

不好的吃飯形象，會讓許多人倒胃口。

公共場合的禮貌（Courtesy in public）

　　老美在公共場所，對個人的公德心和品格修養，也很重視。

Try to be polite, mature and well-groomed in public.

在公共場所，做個有禮貌、明事理、儀表整潔的人。

Don't smoke anywhere that might be offensive to anyone.

任何地方，只要影響到別人，都不可抽菸。

（美國許多州也有法律禁止）

Mind your p's and q's.

注意你的行為和禮節。

（Be careful about your proper behavior and manners.）

Always hold a door open for others when you enter a building or a room.

走進房子時，要把門扶著，讓別人進來。

（有些老中忽視了這點）

Don't show your dislike of a person's dog or cat.

對別人的狗貓，不要表現不喜歡。

（老美把狗貓，視為家裡的一份子）

Don't chew your toothpick in public.

在公共場合，不要在口裡含著牙籤。

Never fail to say sorry if you tread upon or stumble against someone.

如果不小心踩到別人的腳，或撞到別人，一定要說對不起。

（tread upon＝step on one's foot; stumble＝bump）
（tread 是踩到，動詞時態：trod, trodden；bump 是撞到）

Try to be a soft-spoken and even-tempered person at all times; don't be rude, crude or irrational.

時時做個談吐溫和，心情平順的人；不要無禮、粗魯或不理性。

（crude＝rough）

Don't drink beer in a public street.

在街上不可喝啤酒。

（這也是美國的法律）

Don't stare or laugh at any person's disability, peculiarity of manner or dress.

遇到殘疾者或行為衣冠古怪，不可盯著人家看或嘲笑。

Don't taste any food or fruit in the store before paying for it.

商店裡的食品或水果，沒有付錢前不可試吃。

A person's appearance carries great weight. The key is to be well-groomed.

一個人的外表很重要；主要是衣冠清潔整齊。

We never see if a person's mind is blank or a mint of knowledge, but we will not forget if he / she is pleasing to your eyes.

我們看不見一個人是否胸無點墨或學富五車，但我們不會忘記人家賞心悅目的印象。

（a mint of＝a lot of）

Try to be more "street smart" than "book smart."

一位有實際生活經驗而機警生存頭腦的人要比死讀書的人好些。

(street smart 意思是 knowledge about things in life; book smart 是指 knowledge from reading)

Don't be servile toward superiors or arrogant toward inferiors.

對高官富翁，不必卑躬屈膝；對下屬人物也不可傲慢自大。

Don't scold your children or your house maid (or nanny) before others.

不可在他人面前責罵你的孩子或管家／保姆。

A person of (good) breeding never raise his / her voice in an argument.

有好教養的人，不會在爭吵時抬高嗓門。

Using bad language will cheapen yourself. Never yell at anyone else.

用髒話會貶低自己，不可對任何人高喊大叫。

Don't show ill temper if the game goes against you.

如果運動比賽對你不利，不要表現生氣。

It is considered impolite to ask American friends to remove their shoes before entering your home.

進門時，叫老美朋友脫鞋，是不禮貌的。

(一般老美沒有進門脫鞋的習慣)

Don't just drop in and be a self-invited guest; you need to make an appointment first.

不要做不速之客，應該先預約。

Don't wear out your welcome by staying too long at your friend's house.

不要住朋友家住得太久，以免使人厭煩。

Don't be a braggart; let other people find your good points.

不要自吹自擂；讓別人去發現你的優點。

（brag 是動詞，意思是吹牛；動詞時態：bragged, bragging）

Try to put anger or bitterness behind you and behave civilly to others.

把憤怒和痛恨丟在你的腦後，以禮貌對待他人。

Try to be agreeable and go with the flow.

盡量遵照別人的意思去做，隨和別人。

（go with the flow 意思是 easy-going）

Never spit on the sidewalk or street anywhere; spitting is inexcusable.

千萬不可在人行道或任何路上吐痰。吐痰是不可原諒的。

Don't wear pajamas and slippers in public.

在公共場所不可穿睡衣或拖鞋。

Don't talk at a theater or at a concert when the performance is going on.

在電影院或音樂會裡，當節目進行時不可談話。

When a person holds a door for you, don't sail right through without looking at him / her and saying thank you.

當有人為你扶著門，不要輕快地走過，而沒有看著他／她說句謝謝。

Don't offer to shake hands with a woman unless she first extends her hand.

不要先與女士握手，除非她先伸手。

We can disagree on issues, but still like each other.

我們在議題上可以不同意，但還可以彼此喜歡。

Don't neglect the nose hairs that project from the nostrils.

不要讓鼻毛從鼻孔露出。

(project＝stick out)

You only have one chance to make a good first impression.

你只有一個機會贏得第一次好印象。

Try to greet everyone with an engaging smile.

對每個人要露出願意與他／她談話的笑容。

(engaging＝willing to talk)

Many Americans seem friendly and likable at least on the surface.

許多老美至少在表面上顯得友善可愛。

Don't be small and narrow-minded or fight over trifles.

不要胸襟狹窄，為小事而爭。

Never twist your friend's need to fit yours.

不要把你朋友的需要，扭轉成為你的需要。

Don't use judgmental words such as stupid, naughty, disgusting or asinine, etc.

不要使用自我判斷的字眼，諸如呆頭呆腦的、頑皮的、令人作嘔的、愚笨的等等。

Don't use any low-down, vulgar or filthy language.

不要用任何低賤、下流或骯髒的言語。

Don't earn a reputation of busybody or nosy Parker; other person's private life is none of your business.

不要因為好管閒事而出名；別人的私事與你無關。

（busybody＝always interest in others' business 與 nosy Parker 意思相似。Parker 係人名，故要大寫）

Look for the good in everyone and comment on it. Everyone appreciates being complimented sometimes.

在每個人的身上找出優點，並加以讚美。人人都喜歡有時受到誇獎。

Never be a freeloader; always try to invite your friends back to dinner.

不要成為一位吃白食的人；也要回請你朋友吃飯。

(動詞 freeload 是吃白食，佔便宜)

Be sincere to your friends; don't tell them in a roundabout way.

真誠地對待朋友，不必繞圈子說話。

(in a roundabout way＝beat around the bush)

Don't show your super-knowledge by talking above the heads of others. Simplify a complicated topic to let even an uneducated person understand.

不要表現你超高知識而使人滿頭霧水。應該簡化複雜的問題，讓沒有受教育的人也能明白。

It would be nice if we would give praise when it is due.

適當給些誇獎，也是好事。

(when it is due＝if it is appropriate)

Don't encourage friends who walk by to join you in line.

排隊時，不要讓過路朋友插隊。

Don't look for someone in line with whom to strike up a conversation and use that as an opportunity to avoid taking your rightful place at the back of the line.

不要在排隊裡找個熟人說話，借機插隊以避免應該排在後面。

Don't be impulsive and impatient or restless with mood swings and a short temper.

不要因為情緒不定或脾氣大，而顯得容易激動、不耐煩或焦躁不安。

Being a good listener will do more for you than being a good talker; people enjoy talking about themselves and what they are into.

對你來說，做個好聽者，要比多話者好；人們喜歡談談自己所作所為。

(they are into＝they are doing)

Don't show off or put your friend down. Friends should build up and support each other in time of need.

不要炫耀自己而貶低朋友。需要時，朋友應該彼此鼓勵和支持。

Don't overshadow your boss; don't belittle your subordinates.

不要使你的老闆顯得不重要，也不要小看你的部屬。

We should care more about one another rather than about political leanings.

我們應該彼此多關心，不必為了政治傾向而影響。

To hear a different side of the story is a positive step.

聽聽另一方面的意見，是一種積極性的步驟。

Try to approach a person tactfully so that he / she will not reject your idea.

用圓通得體的方式對待他人，這樣人家也許不會拒納你的意見。

One who gives should not remember; one who receives should never forget.

為別人奉獻不必記得；受別人幫助不要忘記。

Try to make every effort to be agreeable and objective.

盡量做個隨和和客觀的人。

Never treat others in a despicable manner. Try to be well-liked and well-mannered.

不要用卑鄙的態度對待別人。做個令人喜歡和舉止親切的人。

Don't be cold, distant, gushing or effusive. A cordial yet quiet manner is the best.

做人不必冷淡疏遠，說話也不必滔滔不絕，或過分的熱情。真誠而溫和的態度是最上策。

（gushing 是亂說話或裝腔作勢；effusive 是過分熱情）

If you attend a party, try to mark the occasion with some sort of gift.

假如你參加一個宴會，最好帶點禮物以表慶賀。

Americans generally will not appreciate advice or help that is not asked for.

老美通常對於沒有請求的忠告或幫忙不領情。

也就是：You advice will fall on deaf ears.

你的忠告將成耳邊風。

You have to say, "Excuse me", when you belch within hearing distance.

當別人可以聽見你打嗝時，要說「抱歉」。

Don't listen in on the conversation of others.

不要偷聽別人的談話。

Try to focus on the positive and count your blessing.

把注意力集中在積極性方面，也要感謝上天的賜福。

 ## 委婉或禮貌用語（Euphemism or fancy, courteous words）

　　老美為了表示談吐斯文雅緻，喜歡說些別人愛聽的話。雖然虛而不實，但會使人感到莊嚴（feel more dignified）。也有人稱為虛誇或言過其實的字眼（pompous or bloated terms），例如：

Both Mr. A and Mr. B are heavy-set persons; they are trying to go on a diet.

A 先生和 B 先生身體都過胖，他們在節食。

（用 heavy-set 代替 fat）(老美認為 fat 是醜，故避免使用，也可用 plus-size 代替 fat：但 heavy-set 較常用）

Mr. A dated a plus-size woman last year.

去年 A 先生與一位胖女人約會。

Even though the saleslady is homely, she seems friendly to her customers.

雖然女店員不漂亮,但她對顧客很友善。

(用 homely 代替 ugly)

Mary is a slim and slender girl.

Mary 是位很瘦小的女孩。

(也可用 thin and petite)(但不用 skinny 或 bony,因為含有瘦得皮包骨的意思)

Mr. B bought an inexpensive gift yesterday for the party.

昨天 B 先生參加宴會,買了一件不貴的禮物。

(用 inexpensive 代替 cheap)(因為 cheap 有劣質或低劣的意思)

His father passed away five years ago.

他父親五年前去世。

(用 passed away 代替 died)

Ed finally decided to put the sick dog to sleep.

Ed 最後決定把病狗安樂死。

(to put an animal to sleep 代替 to kill an animal)

The woman showed the girl where the powder room is located.

那位女士告訴女孩廁所在哪裡。

（用 power room 代替 toilet）

You would find some panhandlers in a big city.

你在大城市可以發現一些乞丐。

（用 panhandler 代替 beggar）

Mr. A has been working as a sanitation engineer.

A 先生是一名垃圾工人。

（用 sanitation engineer 代替 garbage collector）

Mr. B works as a culinary artist at this restaurant.

B 先生在這餐館裡擔任廚師。

（用 culinary artist 代替 cook 或 chef）或：

Mr. B has been good at the culinary arts.

B 先生對烹飪很高明。

（culinary arts 代替 cooking and baking）

Mr. C is between jobs at the moment.

C 先生目前失業。

（用 between jobs 代替 out of job 或 unemployed）

The boy was very sick and threw up everything he ate.

這男孩生病了，吃了什麼都吐出來。

（用 to throw up 代替 to vomit）

Many young people make whoopee in their cars.

許多年輕人在車子裡做愛。

（用 make whoopee 代替 make love）

Mr. A, our school custodian, always arrives around six o'clock in the morning.

A 先生是我們學校工友，他每天早上都是 6 點左右到達。

（用 custodian 代替 janitor）

Mr. B will see a doctor for his two-week irregularity.

B 先生兩星期大便不通，要看醫生。

（用 irregularity 代替 constipation）

He did not know what caused his irregular bowel movement.

他不曉得為什麼大便不正常。

（大便用 bowel movement, 代替 defecation）

Some women are in bad mood during those days.

有些婦女在來經時情緒不好。

（用 those days 代替 menstruation）

The government will have to help more for the underhoused.

政府對無家可歸者，應該有更多的幫助。

（用 underhoused 代替 homeless）

Many African American are good at the performing arts.

許多美國黑人擅長舞台表演藝術。

（用 African American 或 Afro-American 代替 Negro）
（不可再叫黑人為 Negro）

The charity organization has been helping the disadvantaged children.

慈善機構在幫助貧窮的小孩。

（用 disadvantaged 代替 poor）

The bank is working on some nonperforming assets.

這個銀行正在處理一些不良的貸款。

（用 nonperforming asset 代替 badloan）

The store manager is concerned about some inventory shrinkage.

商店經理關心偷竊的事。

（用 inventory shrinkage 替代 theft）

註：

(1)以上所述的生活禮節，都是中、外一般受過教育，品德良好者應有的條件。雖然世上還有許多不講禮貌的人，但是大家都希望做到文明禮貌的地步。

(2)由於老美重視「個人隱私」和「獨立自主」，不喜歡別人常去「打擾」。老中所謂「禮多人不怪」，也要適可而止。

(3)誇獎老美，也不可過分，以免被認為「不誠懇」。

(4)咱們老中在國外，每位都代表全中國人的形象。只要大家知道「自尊而後人尊，自敬而後人敬」的道理，做個「不卑不亢」的老中，才是下策。

(5)文中有些也許老中認為芝麻小事，微不足道，但老外卻很重視呢！

Chapter 2

老美怎樣祝賀親友

　　美國人遇到親友的特別場合，諸如結婚、生日、畢業、升官、退休以及某種成就時，往往只是寄張賀卡或寫封簡短的信，表示心意。

　　雖然賀卡上也印有祝賀的字句，老外通常親筆寫上幾個字以表親切。

　　以下舉些常用的簡單實用字句。如要節省時間，少傷腦筋，也可從中挑選，派上用場。

　　（句中主詞的單複數和動詞的時態，都可加以改變）

 ## 晉升或表揚的祝賀語

My hearty congratulations on your promotion. No one could deserve it more.

我真誠地祝賀你晉升，沒有人比您更應得這個頭銜。

I am very happy to hear of your promotion. I hope it is just one of many more.

我真高興得知您的晉升，我希望這只是許多晉升中之一。

On this joyful occasion I offer my congratulations on your new post as the president of our company.

在這快樂的場合裡，我為您榮任我們公司總裁的新職而祝賀。

Please permit me to congratulate you on your being promoted as director of this department.

請允許我為您升為本部門的主任而道賀。

I think you and your family are about to burst out with joy over your big promotion.

我想您和府上諸位，都會為您的大升遷而極度歡樂。

It's a great pleasure to send you our sincere congratulations on your new appointment.

我很高興為您的新職表達至誠的祝賀。

We congratulate you on your new post and appreciate your decades of service to our school.

我們恭喜你的新職，並感謝您數十年來對本校的服務。

Our hearty congratulations on your being the new chairperson of the committee.

我們真心地祝賀您擔任委員會的新主席。

I know how delighted you must be at the news of your new appointment. I believe your new job will prove challenging.

我知道您對您的新職一定很高興，相信您的新工作具有挑戰性。

It is a thrilling news to hear of your being appointed as CEO of your company.

知道您被任命為貴公司的執行長，是件令人興奮的消息。

I could not let this happy occasion go by without congratulating you: you are a man of achievements.

我怎能錯過在這個歡樂的場合向您祝賀，您是位有成就的人。

My heartiest congratulations on your being named this year's Outstanding Professor of Maryland.

衷心地恭喜您被選為本年度馬里蘭州的傑出教授。

Hats off (to you) and congratulations on a great job. I am so proud of your accomplishment.

讓我向您脫帽致敬。我為您的成就感到驕傲。

(hats off 後面的 to you 可省去)

I am very glad to learn of your winning the blue ribbon in the writing competition.

我很高興得悉您在寫作競賽中贏得冠軍。

Congratulations on your job well done!

恭喜您的工作完美成功。

Congratulations not only on your achievement but also on your fine work over the past years.

不但要恭喜您的成就，也要恭喜您過去多年來美好的工作。

How happy I was to hear that you have won the prize. Hats off and good luck to you.

我多麼高興聽到您得獎的消息。謹向閣下致敬並祝好運。

We would like to express our pride in your accomplishment and extend to you our best wishes for your continued success and happiness.

我們對你的成就感到驕傲，並祝福您繼續成功和幸福。

Please accept my sincere congratulations for this award which honors you for your outstanding public record.

對您優異的大眾服務紀錄而獲獎，請接受我至誠的祝賀。

We are delighted to have read in the newspaper about your award.

我們很高興看到報上刊登有關您得獎的消息。

Congratulations on your receiving the achievement award. I was so delighted for you.

恭喜您獲得成就獎，我真為您高興。

My family join me in offering you our hearty congratulations and best wishes.

我家人和我向您表達衷心的道賀和最好的祝福。

Our heartfelt congratulations on your landslide election. We are pleased to have been a part of your victorious campaign.

我們衷心恭喜您在選舉中大獲全勝。我們很高興能參與您勝利的競選。

Heartiest congratulations on your new book which I have read with fervor and admiration.

衷心恭喜您的新書問世，我已以至誠欽佩的心拜讀大作。

(fervor＝fervour 熱誠)

With admiration, respect and affection, I wish you the best of anything.

懷著欽佩、恭敬和愛慕之心，我祝您萬事好運。

My best wishes for your continued success in all that you undertake.

對您所承擔的一切，我祝福您繼續成功。

The prize you have won is just the beginning of many honors that you will attain in the future.

您所獲得的獎賞，只是您將來許多榮譽的開始。

May God fill your heart with gladness and cheer you every day.

願上帝以喜悅充滿您的心，天天讓您高興。

Kudos to you; you richly deserve the recognition.

恭喜您得獎：這是您應得的報償。

I am sure all your friends are delighted to know that you have been properly rewarded.

我相信您的朋友都會為您榮獲獎勵而高興。

May the success of your first ten years lead to an even more successful second ten.

願您第一個 10 年的成就，帶給您第二個 10 年更大的成就。

May your goodness be like gold, lasting for thousands of years.

願您的美德如同黃金，持續千年。

It must be a great satisfaction to have achieved such a goal.

能達到這樣的目標，一定是很大的滿足。

With best wishes for fair weather and smooth sailing in the years ahead.

祝福您一帆風順，春風得意。

Thank God for honest, decent people like you who go about doing good.

感謝上帝有你這樣誠心善意的好人，到處行善。

You are exceptionally modest about your achievements.

閣下對您自己的成就，是罕見的謙虛。

I know you will go very far in this world. My best wishes for a bright and happy future.

我知道您的前途無量，祝您有個光明幸福的未來。

It's a thrill to see you rewarded for your talent and hard work.

由於您的才華和努力而得獎，是件令人十分興奮的事。

You certainly deserved this award. Your industry and creativity have been an inspiration to us.

您的確值得這份獎賞，您的勤奮和創造力對我們是種鼓舞。

I can't envision anything more satisfying and gratifying than what you have been doing.

我難以想像什麼事比您目前所做的更滿足，更喜悅。

Your civility and approach ability have translated into your popularity.

您那和藹可親及平易近人的態度，使您深得人心。

May these first twenty-five years of success serve as the inspiration for the next twenty-five.

願這前 25 年的成功，做為後 25 年的鼓舞。

I can't tell you how delighted I am, and how proud to have had even a humble association with such a distinguished person like you.

我很難告訴您我是多麼高興，多麼得意能與您這位傑出的人物，頗有交往。

You deserved the award for your exemplary coordination, planning and leadership beyond the call of duty.

您該得這份獎勵，因為您的協調、計畫和領導，都有示範性，且超乎職責。

We are fortunate to have a wealth of people like you who are dedicated to making this community a better place to live.

我們很幸運有像您這樣的一群人，獻身使這個社區成為更好的住處。

I very much admire your achievements, ingenuity and calm in the face of difficulties.

我很欽佩您的成就、才智以及面臨困難時的沉著。

Your step forward as the new CEO of your company is more than deserved.

閣下挺身而出擔任貴公司執行長，是太值得了。

Well done! This is the best news I have heard. Your expertise and creativity have benefited all of us.

幹得好！這是我聽到最好的消息。您的專門知識和創造能力，使我們大家受益良多。

Your report was well-written and highly convincing. You have topped everyone in this department.

您的報告寫得很棒，也有高度說服力，您在本單位處於眾人之上。

It speaks volumes about the wonderful people like you who are living in our community.

我們社區裡，住有像你這樣出色的人，是值得讚揚的。

（speak volumes 意思是含意深刻、值得談論＝ a lot to say about）

I admire your perseverance because you have been devoted to this good cause without other's encouragement.

我欽佩您堅持不懈的精神，你沒有他人的鼓勵就獻身這項善行。

You should get the royal treatment for your twenty years of volunteer work.

您 20 年的義工服務應該得到第一流的禮遇。

This award is to recognize your service which has been of great benefit to the happiness, prosperity and moral growth of our community.

這個獎勵是認同您的服務帶給我們社區的莫大幸福、繁榮以及道德提升。

（of great benefit＝beneficial）

You have demonstrated unwavering enthusiasm for teaching and a determination to improve the achievement of your students.

您為教學表露了堅定的熱情，也提高學生改善成績的決心。

You are a source of wisdom and strength for many people.

您是許多人智慧和力量的源頭。

All you wanted out of life was to be of service to your people and to let our children be proud of you.

你一生所要的就是為人們服務，而讓您的兒女以您為榮。

You are a man with extraordinary gifts of leadership and character.

您是位擁有非凡領導才能和高尚品德的人。

You not only embrace responsibility and demonstrate excellence to your subordinates, but also you are a motivational role model.

您不但欣然接受責任，對部屬作出優異表現，同時您也是一位有積極性的行為榜樣。

You have a particular passion for helping others to achieve their dreams.

您有一種特別的熱情，幫助他人達到夢想。

Your are an educator, mentor, role model and inspiration to many people, and you will likely continue to serve as such for generations to come.

您是許多人的教師、輔導員、模範以及鼓舞人心者。想必您會同樣地繼續服務下去。

You are instrumental in unifying people together to get the job done.

您對團結群眾完成工作,能起很大作用。

You are the unsung hero of so many deeds benefiting our citizenry.

您是無名英雄,做了許多有助我們老百姓的事情。

The speech you gave yesterday was insteresting and instructive. I believe all the audience must be as pleased and grateful as I am.

您昨天的演講,既有趣又富啟發性,我相信所有的聽眾,像我一樣地高興和感謝。

We cannot do anything without your kind assistance and efforts.

若沒有您的好心協助和盡力,我們就一無所成。

I am very proud of the job you do every single day. You deserve the accolades and honors for your work.

我為您每天所做的工作,感到驕傲。您應得工作上的獎勵和榮譽。

I have admired you for your hard work in acquiring an advanced degree in your career.

我很佩服您為了事業而努力爭取高學位。

It's a testimony to your high standing in our community. I wish you continued success in your life.

這證明您在我們社區裡的崇高地位。祝福您生活持續成功。

You are a true power behind the throne.

您是真正具有影響力的人。

(true power behind the throne＝really influential person)

You are recognized for your dedication, vision and hands-on approach to leadership.

您的奉獻、眼光和領導能力的實踐方式，都得到了賞識。

(hands-on 是形容詞，親身實踐的)

You are an icon to many, a hero to some and a larger-than-life image on the intellectual scene.

您是許多人的偶像、某些人的英雄、知識界的傳奇典型。

(larger-than-life 是形容詞，英雄或傳奇色彩的)

We would be hard-pressed to find a more experienced, influential, capable or highly respected person like you.

我們要想找到像您這樣經驗豐富、有影響力、能幹的而受到高度尊敬的人，可真不容易。

(hard-pressed 當形容詞，面臨困難的)

生日的祝賀語

Congratulations and best wishes to you. May you have many more happy birthdays.

恭賀您好運連連，願您有更多的快樂生日。

I wish you a birthday that is over-flowing with fun and happiness.

祝您生日洋溢著快樂和幸福。

It's always a great pleasure to say, "Many many happy returns of the day" to a person like you.

向一位像您這樣的人說「福壽無疆，長命百歲」是件十分愉快的事。

（returns 後面 of the day 通常都被省去）

Here is a warm birthday greeting to a great friend who means so much to me.

這是對摯友溫暖的生日祝賀，您對我來說太重要了。

Many many happy returns! I wish I could be with you to share on this joyful occassion.

祝您壽比南山，福如東海！真盼望我能與您共享這個快樂的場面。

May you have many more happy birthdays and always keep your loveliness and charming personality.

祝您有更多快樂的生日；並常保持您那可愛且令人愉快的性格。

I hope your birthday is especially happy; you deserve the best.

我盼望您的生日特別快樂；您應得最好的一切。

Congratulations on your birthday! I hope you have a wonderful time and get everything you want.

恭喜您的生日，盼望您有個極度愉快的時刻，獲得您所要的一切。

I wish you would make known your secret of always staying young.

我盼望您能讓人知道您永保青春的祕訣。

You are one in a million, you mean so much to my family.

您是一位無與倫比的人物，您對我的家人太重要了。

(in a million 後面的 people 被省略，意思是萬中挑一的、無與倫比的＝unusual)

Our friendship is one of the prized possessions in my life and I will treasure it accordingly.

我們的友誼，是我生命中極有價值的財富，於是我很珍惜它。

We want to tell you what a wonderful blessing you are.

我要讓您知道您是上帝美好的恩賜。

Wishing you many joys throughout a beautiful day and a year filled with good health and happiness.

祝福您整天整年充滿健康幸福的喜樂。

You are the most loving and caring person any friend could ever have.

您是夫復何求最可愛最貼心的朋友。

You are a good and giving person; I hope everything in your life is going well.

您是位仁慈而愛付出的人；願您生活一切順利如意。

Your good character and colorful personality have endeared you to many lifelong friends.

您的優良品德、活潑有趣的個性，贏得許多終身朋友的喜愛。

You are an amazingly thoughtful, personable, supportive and caring person to your friends.

您是位非常體貼、討人喜歡、樂於助人和關心朋友的人。

Your are always giving, kind-spirited, good-hearted, generous to a fault and warm. I am so thankful to have you in my life.

您時時做出奉獻、心地善良、宅心仁厚，慷慨不已又熱情。有您在我生命中，我很感恩。

(generous to a fault＝very generous)

There has never been anyone so wonderful as you and there never will be.

從來沒有任何人像您這樣了不起，將來也不可能有。

Your smile could make anyone smile; I like your infectious personality the most of all.

您的歡笑也帶給每個人歡笑；我最喜歡您那種有感染力的個性。

Your pleasing personality helps you make friends easily; your circle of friends reaches far and wide.

您討人喜歡的品格，讓您容易交友。您的交友圈很廣。

You are a remarkable person with outstanding values and a wonderful heart.

您是位具有傑出價值和偉大心腸的出色人物。

You brighten the lives all around you with your wonderful and warmhearted touch.

您以熱心腸的美好格調，照亮周圍的人的生活。

 ## 嬰兒出生的祝賀語

How happy I was to receive the good news that your new baby has arrived.

我多麼高興知道您的新生兒降生的好消息。

So it is a boy! My hearty congratulations.

您生個男孩，我衷心地恭喜您。

I am (was) very glad to learn of the recent arrival of your baby boy.

我真高興得知您最近「添丁」的消息。

Congratulations from the entire Wang family. We wish you joy and happiness in your little daughter.

王家全體成員恭喜您們生了千金,敬祝幸福快樂。

My sincere congratulations to you both on the birth of your little baby.

我真誠地恭喜您們兩位生了寶寶。

I was so pleased to receive the announcement of the birth of little Bob.

我很高興收到小寶寶 Bob 誕生的通知。

I can imagine how cheerful you both must be to have a baby girl.

我能想像您們兩位一定為貴千金出生而興高采烈。

I want to join those who are congratulating you on the arrival of your little son. I send you and your wife my best wishes on this happy occasion.

我要加入祝賀您們寶寶誕生的人群。在這愉快的場合,我向您和夫人致最好的祝福。

I am sure you and your wife are pleased to be proud parents.

我相信您和夫人都很高興成為得意的父母。

I believe you both must be in the clouds and ecstatic about being parents.

我深信您們兩位當了父母，一定是欣喜若狂。

（in the clouds＝very happy 如置雲端）

This note brings you our hopes that all your wishes for your baby come true in full measure.

這封短信獻上我們的祝福，願您們對寶寶的期待都能成真。

（in full measure＝totally）

I am so happy to hear this wonderful news, and I know you both are very proud parents.

我是多麼高興聽到這個好消息；我知道您們是非常得意的父母。

Becoming parents is one of the most thrilling things in the world.

成為父母是世上最令人興奮的事之一。

I know your baby has a great start in life with such fine parents.

我知道您們的寶寶在這麼好的父母關照下，當有很好的生活開始。

My wife and I admire your vigilance as new parents.

我和內人同感讚賞你們做為新手父母的警覺。

（vigilance 是警覺性，也就是 watchfulness and care about baby's well-being）

Please let us know when is the best time to see the baby.

請告訴我們什麼時間看望寶寶最好。

Lilly and I can't wait to see your little baby when you bring her home.

莉莉和我等不及在你和嬰兒返家後看到他。

Please give our love to the little one, and we will be coming to see the baby whenever his lucky parents feel it's convenient.

請代向小寶寶表示我們的愛意。只要您們這對幸運的父母覺得方便之時，我們就來看望寶寶。

 # 訂婚的祝賀與恭維語

We are delighed beyond words to hear about your engagement.

您們的訂婚消息，使我們高興得難以言語形容。

What wonderful news to learn of your engagement to Miss A.

您與 A 小姐訂婚，是件多麼棒的消息。

It was certainly welcome news that you have made your engagement official.

您已正式宣布訂婚，實在是受人歡迎的消息。

Congratulations to you and best wishes to you and your financee.

恭喜、恭喜；並向您和您的未婚妻致最好的祝福。

（fiance 是未婚夫，與 fiancee 發音不同）

Your life will never be boring when you marry Miss B.

您與 B 小姐結婚，生活不會乏味無聊。

I am so glad to know the news of your engagement and wish you both all happiness and good health.

我很高興得知您們訂婚的消息，並祝您們幸福健康。

I can't tell you how happy I was made by the announcement of your engagement.

您們的訂婚通知，我很難告訴您我是多麼的興奮。

Our hearty congratulations on your engagement!

我們衷心祝賀您訂婚。

 ## 結婚和結婚紀念日的祝賀與恭維語

I was delighted to learn of your marriage.

我真高興知道您們結婚。

Three cheers for you! The good news of your marriage has just arrived.

恭喜！剛剛收到您們結婚的好消息。

(three cheers for you＝congratulations)

I would say you have struck gold! I am looking forward to your wedding.

您很幸運找到良伴。我期待著參加您們的婚禮。

（動詞 strike 是打中，時態是 struck, struck 或 stricken）

Our heartiest congratulations! Please give our best wishes to your bride. We are sure you two will have a very happy life together.

我衷心的恭喜您們。請代向新娘致最好的祝福。我們相信您們兩位共同生活，幸福無比。

（這裡的 life 用單數，是集合名詞，指夫婦共同的生活）

I am sending you and the bride my best wishes for a lifetime of happiness.

我向您和新娘致最好的祝賀，願您們終生幸福。

My warmest congratulations. I wish you a long and fulfilling marriage.

謹致最熱誠的道賀；我祝您們婚姻長久如意。

We hope you and your bride will be happy forever and ever.

我們希望您和新娘永遠幸福。

（forever 後面加 ever，加強語氣）

I am sure he must be a Prince Charming. Otherwise you would not have chosen him.

我相信他一定是白馬王子，否則妳不會選他。

（Prince Charming 也有人小寫 prince charming）

I know how happy you must be as you two are meant for each other.

我知道您們一定非常高興，因為您們是天作之合。

(are meant for each other＝match nicely)

It's the real compliment to you that Miss A decided to marry you. With her personality and loveliness, she'll make you very happy.

A 小姐決定嫁給您是真正的恭維。以她的可愛和個性，她會讓你十分幸福。

The bride is the most amazing and resilient woman I have ever known.

新娘是我所認識的最讓人驚喜和富有活力的女性。

Please give your new husband our hearty greetings; we wish you both all the joy and happiness in the world.

請向您的新婚先生致上我們的衷心祝賀；敬祝您們享有世上所有的歡樂和幸福。

We are sending our best wishes to both of you for your future joy, health and happiness.

我們為您們兩位將來的喜樂、健康、幸福，致最好的祝福。

All best wishes to you both for much health, happiness, prosperity and many more years of togetherness.

祝福您們兩位健康、幸福、成功，並且長相廝守。

We wish you many happy years together surrounded by loving relatives and friends.

我們祝福您們長年快樂，被愛你們的親朋好友圍繞。

A good loving couple like you will always be considered as a blessing.

像您們這樣一對相愛的夫妻，總被視為上帝的賜福。

Congratulations and may there be nothing but the best in store for you both.

恭喜！願兩位擁有世上最好的一切。

(the best in store＝greatest or most helpful)

We wish you every happiness as you celebrate the love you share.

當您們慶祝彼此相愛時，我們也祝您們時時刻刻幸福。

I give you both my blessing and send you my warmest wishes for a long life of happiness together.

我向兩位道賀並致最熱誠的祝福。願您們百年好合。

My sincere congratulations and my best wishes to you both for many happy years ahead.

我至誠地恭喜您們；並祝您們兩位將來有更多的幸福歲月。

Our blessings are upon both of you and wish you happiness every hour, every day and every year.

我們祝福您們兩位，也盼望您們每小時、每天和每年都幸福。

May you and your adoring spouse have many more happy, healthy years together.

願您和您親愛的另一半，同享更多幸福健康的歲月。

May your relationship continue to be a blessing to both of you.

願您們的愛情依然是上帝賜給您們的福氣。

Congratulations on your wedding anniversary. Let's all celebrate this special occasion.

恭喜您結婚紀念日；讓我們一起慶祝這個特別的場合。

May you enjoy many more wedding anniversaries, each happier than the last.

願您們享受更多的結婚紀念日，一次比一次更幸福。

Best wishes for a happy (wedding) anniversary to a couple we have long admired and loved.

謹向我們長期羨慕的賢伉儷，致上結婚紀念日最好的祝福。

Your anniversary is a day for you to celebrate your love, and a day to wish you all the happiness you both so richly deserve.

您們的結婚紀念日是慶祝相愛的日子；也是祝賀您們應得幸福的時刻。

My hat's off to you! My heartiest congratulations to you both. My thoughts are with you today as you celebrate your anniversary.

我向您致敬！我衷心祝賀您們。今日當您們慶祝結婚紀念日時，我的心也與您們同在。

We congratulate you on your tenth（wedding）anniversary. We believe a feeling of contentment and pride must have been brought to you as you shared many beautiful years of togetherness.

我們恭喜您們結婚十周年紀念。相信您們多年來共享美好的生活時，也會感到滿足和得意。

May you have joy and happiness in your life together.

願您們共同生活愉快幸福。

 ## 畢業的祝賀與恭維語

Congratulations on your being graduated from high school.

恭喜您高中畢業。

（美國人對高中畢業很重視）

I am sure you will make a success in your chosen field in college.

我相信你會在大學所選專業成功。

We acknowledge that your superb formation in high school will well prepare your college studies.

我們了解你在高中的傑出過程將是你在大學研究的良好準備。

It was great news to have learned of your graduation from Stanford （University）.

您從史丹福大學畢業，真是一大消息。

Our warmest congratulations on your graduation from Harvard Business School.

您從哈佛大學商學院畢業，我們致上至誠的祝賀。

My wife and I congratulate you on your hard work and dedication in obtaining your college degree.

內人和我恭賀您的努力和專心而獲得大學學位。

It's with great pride that we celebrate your graduation from an Ivy League University.

我們帶著至高驕傲的心情，慶祝您從常春藤大學畢業。

My family join me in sending you our hearty congratulations on your graduation.

為您的畢業，我與家人獻上衷心的祝賀。

I know that in your chosen field of business administration you'll make your mark.

我知道您會在選擇的工商管理領域成功。

（mark＝success）

We would like to express our pride in your academic accomplishments and extend our best wishes for your continued success in all you are undertaking.

我們為你的學術成就感到驕傲。謹致最佳祝福，願您從事一切繼續成功。

It is a wonderful feeling to have reached such a milestone.

能達到這樣的里程碑 ，一定感覺愉快。

You have good reasons to be proud of yourself and your family members have good reasons to be proud of you.

您有理由，感到自豪；您的家人也有理由，以您為榮。

I know your profession needs many more people with your excellent academic achievements.

我知道在你的行業需要更多像您這樣學術成就傑出的人。

Keep up your good record. Your future looks bright from all angles.

繼續保持您的好紀錄。各角度看來，您的前途光明。

I am sure you'll put to good use the knowledge you have gained.

我相信您會好好使用您所獲得的知識。

May the sun always shine in your windowpane.

願陽光時時照在您的玻璃窗上。

(就是「祝您幸福好運」之意)

From your excellent records in school, I am certain you'll be successful in whatever career you pursue.

以您學校的傑出成績來看，我深信不論您從事任何行業，都會成功。

I have high hopes, high in the sky apple pie hopes for your success.

我對您的成功有很高的期望，也就是十全十美的希望。

（high in the sky apple pie＝perfect，只是加強語氣）

I know you have many wonderful, exciting experiences ahead of you both intellectually and romantically.

我知道您將來在知識上和愛情上都會有許多非凡得意的經驗。

We are sure you will keep up your fine achievements in the larger world that is waiting for you.

我們深知您會繼續保持良好成就。寬闊無邊的世界正等著您。

Thinking of you at graduation, I extend my best wishes for your health, happiness and prosperity.

在您畢業時刻想到您，我為您的健康、幸福、成功獻上最好的祝福。

 ## 聖誕／新年的祝賀語

　　因為聖誕新年賀卡上，印有許多祝賀語，在此只舉幾個象徵性的例子。

I wish you and all of your family members continued good health and prosperity.

我祝福您和府上繼續健康和興旺。

We hope this year has started off well and will be one of your best.

我們希望今年有好的開始，也是您最好的一年。

My wish for you is a joyful holiday with family and friends and a peaceful happy New Year.

我祝福您和府上親友們佳節愉快，新年平安快樂。

Holiday blessings to all of you! Wishing you a season of hope, love and joy.

祝福大家節日快樂，願您們佳節充滿希望、愛心和喜悅。

May you and your home be filled with the warmth and love of the holiday season.

願您和府上的佳節裡充滿溫暖和愛。

Wishing you beautiful winter moments and a New Year filled with happiness and joy.

祝您有個美麗的冬天時刻和充滿幸福快樂的新年。

I extend my warmest wishes to you for a joy-filled and bountiful season.

我祝您有個充滿喜樂和富裕的佳節。

May you be inscribed and sealed for a happy, healthy and prosperous year.

願您有個幸福、健康和繁榮的一年。

My wife and I wish you all the best in the coming year surrounded by your loving relatives and friends.

內人和我盼望您在四周的親朋好友中，享有新年最好的一切。

 ## 退休的祝賀語

Retirement may change many things in your lifestyle, but nothing can change the wonderful person you are.

退休也許能改變您生活方式的許多方面，但無法改變您這位非凡的人物。

We will miss your lively and entertaining remarks about life and thought, but we wish you peace and happiness in your retirement years.

我們會懷念您對生活和思想上活潑有趣的看法，但祝福您的退休歲月裡安寧幸福。

Hope you'll soon discover new ways to enjoy each day with all the pleasure and the rewards of being your own boss.

希望您很快找出新方式，使您每天能享受當自己老闆的愉快與報償。

Bravo! You will not allow age to hold you back.

恭喜！您不會讓您的年齡阻撓您。

（Bravo 本是喝彩聲＝congratulations）

Every wrinkle and laugh line has been well-earned.

每一個皺紋和笑紋都是富有代價的。

(通常對好友才會提到，因為一般老外不願外人提醒臉上的皺紋。)

Along with your well-deserved retirement, you also deserve a big thank-you from all of us.

您除了理所當然的退休外，也值得我們大家一個大大的感謝。

I wish you contentment, relaxation and all other good things during your retirement years.

我祝福您在退休的歲月中，享有滿足、輕鬆和其他美好的事物。

While working people are fiercely competitive, you can remain now a consummate gentleman.

當上班族還在爭個你死我活時，您現在就能保持完美的紳士氣派。

I know you, as a retiree, will continue to be a person of ideals, principles, intelligence and refinement.

您做為一位退休者，我知道您會繼續是位有理想、原則、智慧和教養的人物。

老闆日的祝賀語

　　老美通常不送老闆禮物，以免有賄賂、拍馬屁之嫌。不過，遇到好老闆，寄張賀卡，寫幾個字，也算合宜。

Happy boss's day! Thanks for being the boss who keeps me motivated.

老闆日快樂！謝謝您做個讓我積極向前的老闆。

From my heart to yours, you are the greatest boss.

向您說句真心話，您是最了不起的老闆。

Great leaders are ones who know they are the important ones, but act as though they are not.

偉大的領導者是那些知道自己重要的人物，但他們表現得自己不重要似的。

I thank you for being a superb boss.

謝謝您是我第一流的上司。

Respectful, kind, caring and considerate are just a few words that come to my mind to describe you as my boss.

尊重、慈愛、貼心、體貼是我想到的幾個字，能描寫您當我的老闆。

You are 100 percent the best kind of boss I'll ever meet.

您是我所見到百分之百最好的上司。

I haven't met any boss who could top you. Your devotion to helping your subordinates is without equal.

我還未見過任何一位勝過您的上司；您幫助部屬的熱心是無與倫比的。

(top 當動詞用；equal 當名詞＝comparison)

As a boss, you are not only wiser than most, you are also kinder. My hat is off to you.

做為老闆，您不但比多數人聰明，也比較仁慈；我向您致敬。

You are the most down-to-earth boss I have ever known. May your strong and capable hands be always ready to help out.

您是我認識最務實的老闆。願您強壯能幹的雙手，隨時準備好助人一把。

旅遊的祝福語

Have a nice trip!

祝您有個愉快的旅行！

Bon voyage!

祝您旅途愉快！

(bon＝good；本是指乘船旅行，現在用在任何方式的旅遊)＝I hope you enjoy your trip!＝I hope you have a wonderful trip.

I wish you Godspeed!

祝您好運！

＝Good luck for your rtip!（godspeed 也有人小寫）

I wish you good breezes and fair weather.

祝您一路順風，旅途平安！

Come home safe and sound!

願您平安健康歸來。

 ## 送禮客套語

　　老美通常在結婚、生日、畢業時，也會寄些禮物，(也有寄禮券或支票)。老中也常送紅包(現金或支票)。

Enclosed is a small check as a token of our love.

附上一張小小支票，只是象徵性地聊表我們的愛。

In this same mail, I am sending you a little remembrance which I hope you'll enjoy.

在這郵包裡，我寄一點紀念品，希望您會喜歡。

I feel sorry I can't be there to celebrate with you, but I'm sending you a little something in a separate package.

真抱歉，我無法與您一起慶祝，不過我另寄一點東西，聊表心意。

To prove my good intentions, I'm sending to you a small gift. Believe me, I'll be thinking of you on your special occasion.

為了表示我的祝賀，我寄上一點小禮物。請相信我，在這特別的場合，我會想念您。

（這裡的 good intentions＝good wishes）

We are sending you a little gift that we hope you will enjoy. With it go our congratulations and all our affection.

我們寄上一點小禮物，希望您能喜歡；並以我們愛慕之心，向您祝賀。

（it 指 gift）

The enclosed "red-envelope" (hong-bao), gift of good luck, is merely a token of our deep affection for you. It would make us happy if you would buy youself a little something with our small check.

隨信附上一個表示好運的「紅包」禮物，聊表我們對您的關愛。若您能用這張小支票，為自己買點東西，我們也會很開心。

註：老美祝賀或恭維親友都較正式，所以不宜開玩笑（joking），也不必過分熱情，吐露過多（effusiveness）或過分諂媚（flattery）。

Chapter 3

老美怎樣安慰
親友

　　美國人遇到親友心情消沉、失意、煩惱或是生病、車禍、喪事時，通常會說幾句安慰話，或寄張慰問卡，寫上幾句，表示關懷之意。

　　下面是老外通常的一些表達方式，咱們需要時，也可「模仿」一下，或「組合」一封簡短的信，節省一點「絞腦汁」的時間。

　　現在我分幾個不同情況，分別說明。（例句中的主詞、單複數，以及動詞的時態等，都可視情況需要而更改）

 ## 一般情況

　　遇到親友生氣、煩惱、沮喪時，說幾句安慰勸勉的話，可舒緩對方的心情。

　　例如：

I can understand why you are upset.

我能了解你為什麼不高興。

I don't blame you for being mad.

我不怪你生氣。

I guess you are feeling cornered, everyone has that feeling sometimes.

我猜想你在煩惱，每個人有時都會有那種感覺。

(to feel cornered 意思是 in trouble)

What are you fretting about? What can I do to support you?

什麼事讓你煩躁呢？我能為你效勞什麼嗎？

（to fret about＝to worry about）

Talking things over is a good way to solve problem. Do you wish to talk it over?

把事情說開是解決問題的好方法，你想把它說開嗎？

The first thing you must do is to calm yourself.

你第一件要做的事，就是自己要冷靜下來。

You may find some like-minded friends to talk about your problem.

你可找些志同道合的朋友談談你的問題。

（like-minded 是形容詞，意思是志趣相投）

If it is not your worry, just let it lie.

假如不是你的苦惱，就讓它去吧！

（to let it lie＝to let it go）

Don't freak out; it is not the end of the world.

不必過分煩惱，這不是世界末日。

（to freak out＝over-worried 或 over-react）

Worry can only produce frustration, tension and failure.

煩惱只會造成憤怒、緊張和失敗。

（worry 是名詞）

Worry only if and when the problem actually comes up.

只有問題真正發生時，才去操心。

（worry 是動詞）

Our life has its ups and downs and we need someone to ride with us.

在我們的生命中都有得意和失意的時候，我們需要有人的鼓勵和扶持。

（to ride with＝to go along 或 to encourage）

I am here to cheer you up; don't cry at the drop of a hat.

我來這裡是要逗你高興的，不必為小事情而生氣。

（drop of a hat 指小事情，就像掉下帽子一樣，是很平常的事＝don't get upset for minor things easliy）

Cheer up! It could always be worse; it was not as bad as it could have been.

振作起來吧！事情可能更糟，但不是原來想像中那麼糟。

What happened to you has happened to everyone at one time or another.

發生在你身上的事，有時也發生在任何人的身上。

It's better to let off steam and talk about your troubles.

發洩一下激動的情緒，談談你的煩惱，總是好些。

（to let off 或 blow off steam，本是放掉蒸氣，即減少壓力＝to lose emotional stress）

Under the circumstances, your reaction was natural and justified.

在此情況下，你的反應是自然的，而且是正當的。

I can understand that this has caused you a great deal of difficulty and embarrassment.

我了解這件事造成你許多的困擾和尷尬。

He is no gentleman and you don't have to sink to his level.

他不是有教養的人，你不必與他同流合污。

(He is no gentleman. 是口頭語；正式說法是 He is not a gentleman. ; to sink to one's level＝to do what one does)

Don't worry! I am rooting for you.

不必操心！我會你為加油。

(to root for someone，為某人打氣，或支持某人)

Calm you fears; don't panic.

平息你的恐懼，不要驚慌失措。

Let's work out this problem together; we can try to come up with a better solution.

讓我們一同解決這個問題；我們能想出較好的辦法。

Things will get better; it's only a matter of time.

事情會轉好，只是時間問題。

When emotions run high, people often say things they regret.

當情緒激動時，人們會說些後悔的話。

Try to give him some time to cool off and sort out his feelings.

給他一點時間讓他冷靜下來，調整一下他的心情。

Just take it easy; what is done is done, so don't flog yourself.

放輕鬆些，做了就做了，不必太責怪自己。

(to flog 是鞭打＝to beat；動詞時態是 flogged, flogging)
(take it easy，有時告別時，也指「請保重」。it 指任何事情，不能省略。)

We can settle this issue tactfully so it does not fester below the surface.

我們能技巧地解決這個問題，使情況不致變得更糟。

(動詞 fester 是變壞、惡化；festers below the surface 就是 situation gets worse)

There is no rose without a thorn.

沒有不帶刺的玫瑰。(即沒有盡善盡美的生活)

(也就是：Life always has some difficulties.)

If I were you, I probably would be more than willing to let bygones be bygones.

假如我是你，我也許會很願意讓過去的事過去。

(bygone 是形容詞，但 bygones 是名詞；let bygones be bygones 即既往不究
或盡棄前嫌)

Stop beating up on yourself; don't let your past define your future.

不要再責怪你自己，不可讓你的過去，限定你的未來。

(to beat up＝to blame; to define 是下定義，確定界線)

Blowing up is not on the list of ideal ways to communicate with her.

大發脾氣不是與她溝通的理想方式。

Forgive yourself and then re-dedicate yourself.

原諒你自己，再度努力嘗試。

(re-dedicate 就是 try again 或 concentrate harder)

Dry your tears and straighten up!

擦乾眼淚，勇往直前。

(也就是：Stop crying and be brave!)

If you slip up, don't give up.

假如你犯錯，不可自暴自棄。

(to slip up＝to make mistakes)

You should get over it and move on with your life.

你必須度過難關，繼續生活下去。

(to get over 克服困難；to move on 是繼續前進)

Just take steps to ensure that it does not happen again.

只要採取步驟保證此事不會再度發生。

The grass is not always greener on the other side; sometimes it is poison ivy.

另一邊的草，未必比較綠，有時還是毒草呢！

（也就是別人未必都比你好，有時甚至比你還糟呢！）

Don't let yourself be driven by an urge to perfection.

不要讓追求完美的強烈欲望壓迫你自己。

This situation can be mended to everyone's satisfaction.

這個情況可以補救，使每個人都滿意。

Just hang on to your job; don't quit (it) in a huff.

保住你的工作，不可因一時生氣而辭職。

（to hang on to something 緊緊抓住某件事；in a huff 指憤怒或生氣時）

Try not to become combative and defensive when you are being criticized.

當你被人批評時，試著別好鬥或過分防衛。

Don't be disrespectful when someone takes a position contrary to you.

當別人的立場與你不同時，不必表現粗魯無禮。

You must be extremely resilient to have lived with this man all these years.

這些年來，妳能與這種男人住在一起，必然很有適應力。

（resilient 意思是 flexible）

There is plenty of fish in the sea; you can find another man.

（海上的魚多得很，你可以找到另一位男人。）

（也就是世上男人多得是，勸人不必難過。fish 可指男女，機會或工作等。）

Sometimes you will need to hear his side of the story.

有時你也要聽聽他的說法。

It is difficult to be loving to others if you don't love yourself.

如果你不愛自己，就不容易去愛別人。

You don't need more spilled ink; you need to be more careful.

你要避免錯誤，需要更加的小心。

（spilled ink＝mistake 或 setback）

I am confident that you can resolve this problem to your mutual satisfaction.

我相信你能解決這個問題而取得彼此滿意。

This might be the best way to defuse the situation without ending the friendship.

這也許是緩和情況的最好方式而不致結束友誼。

（to defuse 緩和、減少危險）

If he is unwilling to cooperate, then you can help him see the light.

假如他不願合作，你就幫他更充分了解。

（to see the light＝to understand better）

By overcoming your self-destructive tendency, you can achieve a more rewarding and happier life.

你要克服自我損傷的傾向，才能取得較有意義和較幸福的生活。

Once you find a way to contribute constructively to your life, you'll begin to feel better about yourself.

一旦你找到一個對你生命有建設性的貢獻途徑，你就會開始對自己感到滿意。

Your problem will only be compounded if you don't listen to my advice.

如果你不聽我的勸告，你的問題會更複雜。

 生病不舒服

親友生病，通常只是口頭上的簡單慰問或寄張 get-well 的慰問卡，表示關心。雖然卡片上印有慰問字句，但能親筆寫上幾個字，更能顯得親切。

1. 一般開頭語：

例如：

I am sorry to hear about your illness.或 I am sorry to know that you are not feeling well.

聽到你不舒服，我覺得難過。

What a shame that you have been under the weather.

真遺憾，你生病了。

（under the weather 是生病，不舒服）

We are all distressed to hear of your illness.

知道你生病，我們都很牽掛。

I learned only today of your illness and hasten to send you this card / note.

我今天才知道你生病了，所以趕快寄這張卡片給你。

Word has it that your husband has been under the weather.

我聽說你先生不舒服。

（Word has it＝I have heard; word 當集合名詞，故用單數）

I am sorry to know that you have been hospitalized.

得知你住院的消息，我覺得難過。

Your wife has just informed me of your illness and that you'll be forced to stay in the hospital for a few days.

你夫人告訴我你生病了，而且要住院幾天。

2. 一般關心祝福語：

例如：

I hope you will feel better.

我希望你健康起來。

Please get better soon and stay well for keeps.

請趕快好起來，並且一直保持健康。

(for keeps＝always)

Here is wishing that you will be on your feet soon.

盼望你盡快康復。

(Here is wishing that＝I wish that; to be on one's feet＝to get well)

Hurry up and get well! We are very concerned about you.

趕快好起來，我們很關心你。

Cheer up! I just can't have you feeling below par.

提起精神來，我真不要你生病。

(to feel below par，不舒服，在健康水平之下)

We just want to let you know how concerned we are.

我們要你知道，我們是多麼關心你。

Best wishes for your speedy recovery.

祝福你盡速康復。

I hope you will be back to your old self soon.

我希望你很快康復。

(to be (back) to one's old self＝to be back on one's feet＝to get well＝to be healthy)

You have all my best wishes for a full recovery.

我致上最佳的祝福，願你完全復元。

All of us are hoping for your quick return to health.

我們都希望你很快地康復起來。

We are thinking of you and hoping you will be back on your feet in no time.

我們都惦念你，希望你盡速康復。

(in no time＝quickly)

You are very much on my mind and in my heart these days.

這些日子，我都在惦念你，牽掛你。

My wife and I want you to know that you are in our thoughts and in our prayers.

內人和我要你知道，我們都在牽掛你，也為你祈禱祝福。

I wish you a speedier than speedy recovery. Just concentrate on getting well and don't worry about a thing.

願你盡早康復，把精神集中在康復上，不必為任何事苦惱。

We hope there is nothing to keep you from us very long.

我們希望沒有什麼事能讓我們分開太久。

Keep your spirits up! I hope your convalescence progress quickly.

保持你的高昂情緒！希望你很快康復。

（to keep one's spirits up 是提起精神，振作起來；convalescence 康復期）

We are rooting for you to get better very soon.

我們為你加油，願你快速康復。

I hope by the time you receive this message you will be feeling much better.

我希望你收到這個信息時，已經好多了。

With all your pep and energy, I can't imagine you are laid low by the flu for so long.

像你這樣精力充沛的人，我很難想像你竟然得流感而臥病這麼久。

（pep 精力、活力；to be laid low＝to be sick）

I am glad to know that you will not be laid up (for) too long.

我很高興知道你臥病在床不會太久。

（to be laid up＝to be laid low，都是指生病休養，多半用被動語態）

I hope you are in good hands and will soon be back in good health.

我希望你能得到良好的照顧，早日康復。

(to be in good hands 取得良好的照料)

I am relieved to know that your surgery went well and you will regain your health before very long.

知道你手術順利，不久將會康復，我感到寬慰。

You are too nice a person to be out of circulation.

你是位大好人，不能沒有社交活動。

Our office is not the same without you. With best wishes for your full recovery and return to business as usual.

我們辦公室沒有你就是不一樣，祝你完全康復回到正常生活。

By the time this note reaches you, I hope you are feeling much better. Please let me know how I can be of service to you.

當你收到這個短訊時，我希望你好多了。我如何能為你效勞，請告知。

We are all hoping and praying for your speedy recovery. We are looking forward to your coming home soon.

我們都在祈求上帝祝福你早日康復，並期待你盡速回家。

What pleasant news it was to learn of your great improvement since your surgery. It will do you a world of good just resting and getting back your strength.

聽到你手術後大有進步，真是好消息。只要好好休息，恢復精力，那是對你最好的事。

Our thoughts are with you to keep you company along with happy wishes for your full recovery.

我們的關懷與你同在，祝你完全康復。

As soon as you feel stronger, we can get together and lift a few beers.

一旦你稍微強壯，我們就能相聚一堂，把酒歡樂。

If a brief visit from me and my wife will bring you a little cheer, please let me know.

如果我和內人的短暫拜訪，能逗你開心一點，請告知。

（一般在病人不願朋友看望、打擾的情況下使用。）

 ## 車禍或火災

　　遇到朋友發生這種意外事故時，也可寄張卡片，親筆寫上兩句，表示慰問。

1. 一般開頭語：

例如：

Your wife has just told me about your car accident. I feel sorry to hear about it.

你夫人剛才告訴我有關你車禍的事，聽了很難過。

I am sorry to learn of your car accident, but I am relieved to know your injuries are not serious.

知道你發生車禍，我很難過，不過可以寬慰的是你的傷勢不重。

I have just heard about the car accident which sent you to the hospital.

我剛聽到車禍讓你住院的消息。

John just told me about your distressing accident, but I am glad to know that your injuries are less serious than they might have been.

John 剛剛告訴我關於你的意外事故，但我感到安慰的是你的傷勢不嚴重，比想像中好得多。

(they 指傷勢)

I want you to know how sorry I am to learn of the fire which destroyed your home.

知道你的房子被大火焚毀，我是多麼的難過。

2. 一般安慰的話：

例如：

I hope you'll be out of the hospital in no time. My family joins me in sending our best wishes for your swift recovery.

我希望你很快出院；我家人和我都祝你早日康復。

I know you will be as good as new when you come out from the hospital. I am anxious to see you around soon.

你出院後，會像新人一樣的健康，我急盼著你早日出現在我們的周圍。

It is good to know that you are on the mend and will be out of the hospital soon.

真好，知道你逐漸康復，並即將出院。

（to be on the mend 慢慢康復）

I am overjoyed that it would not be long before you are up and around again.

我太興奮了，你能到處走動。

（to be up and around 指病後能到處走動）

Please let me know if there is anything I can do while you are laid up.

你臥病時，我如有效勞之處，請示知。

If I can be of any service during your convalescence, be sure to let me know.

在你康復期間，我如能代勞的事，務必告知。

We are comforted that no one was injured in the fire. We hope you have not lost the accumulation of a lifetime. Please tell us if I can make things easier for you.

我們覺得安慰的是，沒有人在火災中受傷。我們希望你沒有失去一些所保存的東西。如有什麼事，我能讓你順利度過難關，請告知。

※其他例句與上面生病的「關心祝福語」相似。

 ## 親友的喪事

遇到親友喪事時，向其家人說句安慰話，或寄張 Sympathy 的慰問卡，親筆加上幾個字，也可顯得親切些。

參加喪禮時，可向親友的家人說：

My heart goes out to you and your family.

我以誠摯的心，向你和府上諸位致慰問之忱。

I am so sad about your loss. My thought is with you.

我對你的損失非常難過；我一直牽掛著您。

I am sorry this happened; life is sometimes unfair.

發生這樣的事，我很難過；生命有時是不公平的。

I have lost a very dear and valuable friend. Mr. A will always remain in my thought.

我失去一位敬愛和珍貴的朋友；我會時常懷念 A 先生。

I will miss John very much. You are in my prayers.

我會十分想念 John；我會為你祈禱祝福。

I am thinking of you every minute and sharing your grief.

我時時刻刻都在惦念你，並且分擔你的悲傷。

In this sad hour, my heart is with you. If there is anything I can do, please count on me.

在這悲痛之時，我的心與你同在。如有效勞之處，我是可以信賴的。

1. 一般開頭語：(可用在安慰卡上或短信上)

例如：

It came as a tremendous shock to me that Mr. A passed away.

A 先生的去世，給我極大的震撼。

I was shocked and distressed to learn of Mr. A's passing.

得悉 A 先生的去世，我很震驚和悲傷。

I learned just today of the parting of your loved one.

今天我剛知道你珍愛的人永別了。

(passed away＝passing＝parting，都是代替 die 或 death 的委婉語)

We are deeply saddened and shocked at Mr. A's passing.

A 先生不幸去世，我們深表震撼和哀悼。

The sudden passing of your loved one was a great shock to me.

你所愛的人突然去世，對我是個極大的震撼。

The sad news of Mr. A's passing is something that I can still hardly believe.

A 先生去世的不幸消息，我仍然難以相信。

I have just learned with deepest sorrow and regret of the passing of your beloved mother.

我剛知道令堂去世的消息，內心甚感難過和遺憾。

(beloved 可加在朋友的妻子、丈夫或父母之前；而 loved one 多半用在一般朋友)

It was with deep sorrow that I have learned today of the passing of your beloved husband.

今天知道你先生去世的消息，我十分悲痛。

The word of John's sudden passing shocked me.

John 的突然去世，令我震驚。

I know Uncle John's passing has given you a heavy blow.

我知道 John 叔叔的去世，帶給你很大的打擊。

We are all saddened by the loss of your loved one.

你失去心愛的人，我們都很難過。

It was a terrible shock to learn of Mr. A's death (passing).

A 先生的永別，令人莫大的震愕。

2. 一般安慰語：(也可寫在卡片上或短信上)

例如：

I wish to offer my sincere sympathy to you at this time.

此刻我向你致上真誠的哀悼。

I want you to know that you have my affectionate sympathy.

我謹向你致上親切的慰問。

My wife and I offer you our most sincere sympathy in your loss.

你的損失，內人和我向你致上最誠摯的慰問。

I wish to express to you my deep sorrow on the loss of your loved one.

你失去心愛的人，我要表達深切的哀悼。

At this time my thoughts are with you and I hope this note may help a little bit to sustain you.

此刻我很牽掛你，希望這個短訊能帶給你一點支撐的作用。

(to sustain＝to support)

I know you will bear up under this loss with courage and faith.

我知道你能以勇氣和信心，度過這個損失的難關。

Our heart are filled with sorrow for you. There is so little we can do to ease your pain and anguish.

為你，我們內心充滿悲傷。我們很難做些可以減少你痛苦的事情。

Words cannot express my shock and grief at the news of your loss.

對你損失的消息，不是字句可以表達我的震驚和悲傷。

Mr. A's passing (或用 parting) has left a tremendous void in our lives, but we will try to fill it with previous memories of the joy and love we shared.

A 先生的去世，留給我們生活中一大空白，但我們想用過去共享快樂和關愛的美好回憶去彌補。

(passing 比 parting 常用)

Please accept my most profound sympathy for the untimely loss of your loved one.

我為你心愛的人過早去世，致最深切的慰問。

I want you to know that my heart aches for you and your family. May you be given strength to bear this heavy burden.

我要你知道我為你和府上諸位，內心感到十分難過；願你有力量來承受這個重大的負擔。

Words are so inadequate at a time like this, yet please know that my thoughts and prayers are always with you.

在這時刻，任何字句都不足表達，但我為你時時牽掛和祈禱祝福。

I know words offer small comfort in your hours of sorrow. I do wish to extend my hearty sympathy to you on the loss of your beloved wife.

我知道在你悲傷的時刻裡，字句只能給你極少的安慰，但我盼望為你失去心愛的夫人致上至誠的弔慰。

I wish I could find words to tell you how deeply sorry I feel for you in your sorrow.

在你悲傷之時，我盼望我能找出字眼表達我內心的難過。

Please accept my heartfelt sympathy in the bereavement that you have suffered.

在你悲痛之時，請接受我衷心的慰問之忱。

It's my prayer that the love for you may help sustain you in this sad time.

我祈求我對你的關愛，能在此時有點支撐作用。

I feel anything I can say will be futile at this time. My heartfelt sympathy goes to you and your family from the bottom of my heart.

我覺得此時說什麼都是無用的，我謹向你和府上致內心深切的慰問。

My wife and I wish to express our deepest condolence to you and your family on the passing of your beloved mother.

令堂的去世，內人和我向你和府上致最深切的弔慰。

What a difficult task it is to write a note on such an occasion. You and your family have my sincere thoughts of love and condolence.

在這場合要寫幾個字是多麼困難；我謹向你和府上致至誠的愛心和弔慰。

I want you to know how deeply I sympathize with you in your bereavement.

我要你知道，我對你的悲痛致上深切的弔慰。

I know that words cannot console you in your deep sadness. I can only send you my love and hope you will be given strength to bear your sorrow bravely.

我知道言語不能安慰你的悲傷，我只能獻上我的愛心，希望你用毅力勇敢地支撐下去。

I realize how little the words and acts of friends can do to ease the grief that has come to you.

我了解朋友的話語和行動，很難減輕你面臨的悲痛。

My family members join me in expressing our sadness on the passing of your beloved husband.

對你先生的去世，我的家人和我在此表達內心的沉痛。

I am sharing your deep sorrow with you. I stand ready to do anything I possibly can to make your burden perhaps a little easier.

我要分擔你的悲痛；我要盡力做點也許能減少你心中負擔的事。

It's impossible to put into words how I feel. I hope your faith and courage may bring you peace in this deep sorrow.

我內心的感受無法以文字表達。希望在此悲痛之時，你的信念和勇氣，能帶來寧靜與平安。

How can we express enough the sadness we feel for you on the passing of your loved one. My wife and I are all thinking of you and sympathizing in your grief.

對你失去心愛的人，我們很難表達內心的悲傷。內人和我都在惦念你，並對你的悲痛致上弔慰。

Though words are futile, I must tell you how deeply sad I feel for you in this great sorrow.

雖然字句無法表達但我必須告訴你，我對你的悲痛是何等的難過。

3. 一些懷念語

如對死者有所懷念，也可加上兩句讚美語。

例如：

I will always remember him as one of the kindest and most generous person I have ever known.

我會常常記得他是我認識的最慈愛最慷慨的人。

She has achieved high respect and esteem in our community. Her absence will be felt by many in the years to come.

在我們社區裡，她享有崇高的尊敬和評價；她的永別，許多人在將來的歲月裡，都會感受得到。

It was my privilege to enjoy his friendship. His passing is certainly a loss from a personal as well as business standpoint.

我有幸享受到他的友誼，從私人和工作立場來說，他的去世，確是一大損失。

He was a gracious person whose passing will leave our lives a void.

他是位和藹可親的人；他的去世，將留給我們生活上的空白。

Mr. A was a fine man: friendly, considerate and kind. He will not soon be forgotten by many who knew him.

A 先生是位友善、體貼和慈愛的人，許多認識他的人，不會很快忘記他。

I realize how much Mrs. A will be missed in our community for which she did so much.

我體會到我們社區的人都會懷念 A 太太；她為我們做了許多事。

Your mother will be long remembered by many. Her pleasing personality and beauty of her character will leave a lasting impression upon all who knew her.

許多人都會長久記得伯母，她那種令人喜悅的品格以及優美的個性，將留給所有認識她的人一種永恆的深刻印象。

Mr. A has left a place that can never be filled. I felt I never knew a kinder, more friendly person as he was.

A 先生留下的位置，是無法填補的；我覺得我從未認識過一位比他更仁慈、更友愛的人。

I shall always remember his delightful personality, and I realize how great is your loss.

我會常常記得他那令人愉快的性格；我也體會到這是你莫大的損失。

Mr. A was a wonderful person and I will miss him more than I can say.

A 先生是位了不起的人；我對他惦念之情，非言詞可以形容。

It was a joy to work with Mr. A. He brought wit, grace and a great love to his work.

能與 A 先生一起工作是一種享受；他帶來智慧、美德以及對他工作的熱愛。

We found him a delightful and personable person. We consider ourselves blessed to have been his close friends.

他是位令人高興討人喜歡的人，我們有幸是他的好友。

I have heard the highest praise of his character and integrity, no doubt his parting is a great loss to all who knew him.

我聽說他的品格和廉正，受到高度的評價。無疑地，他的去世，對所有認識他的人，都是莫大的損失。

I hope you will find some comfort in the memory that your father was a wonderful man.

令尊是位了不起的人，我希望這種回憶，能帶給你一些慰藉。

He was a great mentor, friend, scholar and role model. I hope the happy memories may make a little easier for the sorrow you have to bear.

他是位良師、益友、學者和他人的榜樣。我盼望美好的回憶，能減輕一點你承受的悲傷。

Mr. A was one of the most remarkable persons I have ever known. He has made an extremely generous contribution to the charity cause.

A 先生是我認識的很出色的人物，他為慈善的事業，做出非常慷慨的奉獻。

After the passing of Mr. A, his words and aspiration will always remain in the minds of many.

A先生去世後，他的言語和志向，將常常留在許多人的心裡。

　　註：(1)老外看望病重的親友，或參加喪事時，都盡量保持
　　　　平靜、嚴肅和理智，不會放聲大哭。(2)寫慰問卡或寫
　　　　短信，老外也是力求簡單，不囉嗦。(3)需要時，可把
　　　　上述不同的例句，稍加「排列組合」成為一封短信。

Chapter 4

老美怎樣寫
謝卡

　　美國人自小開始訓練，養成文明禮貌的習慣，不管別人為你做了什麼芝麻小事，都會說聲（thank you）。尤其遇到朋友送禮、請客招待、或特別幫忙，更會寄張謝卡（或空白卡片），親筆寫上幾個字，表示真誠的感謝。這就是所謂「thank you note」。這對一些不說謝謝（thankless）的人們來說，也有一點「鼓勵」作用。

　　為了節省許多老中的寶貴時間，我把一般謝卡大致分為四類：(1)謝送禮(2)謝招待(3)謝幫忙(4)謝慰問。並舉出例句，做為參考。(句中的主詞，動詞單複數，禮物的名稱，送禮的對象與場合，請客招待和幫忙的種類，都可加以改變)

謝送禮（Thanks for gifts）

　　一般包括結婚、生日、畢業、生小孩、聖誕等等。禮物多半是不貴的生活用品。購買的謝卡，即是印有感謝的字眼，但還要親筆寫上幾個字，表示親切。（老外多半都會在謝卡上指出禮物的名稱和喜愛）

　　例如：

Thank you ever so much for the pretty soft and fluff sweater you bought for me. With the cold weather coming, it is just what I need. How like you to be so generous!

謝謝你買給我那件漂亮柔軟毛衣。天氣即將轉冷，這正是我所需要的。你太大方了！

How thoughtful of you to select such a distinctive oil painting as our wedding gift. You can be sure it will always be one of our most treasured possessions.

你是多麼周到，選一幅如此精美油畫作為我們結婚禮物。相信我，它將是我們最珍惜的家產之一。

A big thank-you for your kindness and thoughtfulness in sending me that beautiful silk scarf from China. You are so observant to know that I love scarves and wear them often. You couldn't have given me a better gift.

感謝你的愛心和體貼，寄給我來自中國的絲圍巾。你真會觀察，知道我愛圍巾，常常使用。你很難給我比這更好的禮物。

You really have a knack in selecting such a beautiful figurine for Christmas. Many thanks for your generosity and good wishes.

你真有本事，能挑選一個這麼漂亮的小塑像，做為聖誕禮物。非常感謝你的大方和祝福。

Bob and I were delighted with your Christmas gift, the luscious smoked ham. We will think of you with every bite we take. Thank you for remembering us so handsomely.

Bob 和我非常喜歡你們送的美味煙燻火腿作為聖誕禮物。我們每吃一口，都會想到你們。謝謝你們這樣地關心我們。

I am simply delighted with the tea set you so graciously presented to me at my retirement last week. It is a beautiful set that I shall always be proud to own. My sincere thanks to each and every one of you.

上周在我的退休歡送會中，你們親切地送我全套茶具，我太高興了。能擁有這麼漂亮的禮物，我很得意。謹向你們每位致上最真誠的謝意。

Your gift was right on target. You must be a mind-reader. We'll think of you every time we use your lovely stainless blender. We were touched by your thoughtfulness.

你的禮物，就是我真正想要的，你一定是位能透視別人心意的人。我們每次用到漂亮的不鏽鋼打果汁機時，都會想到你。你的關心周到，我們很感動。

The jade bracelet from China is one of the most beautiful gifts I have ever received. I shall treasure it all the more because it came from you. Thank you again and again.

來自中國的玉手鐲是我收到最漂亮的禮物之一。因為那是你送的，我會好好珍惜它。再次謝謝。

What a delightful surprise to receive your gift this afternoon. The beautiful dinnerware you sent was something we will treasure for a long time. We appreciate your kindness more than we can say.

今天下午收到你的禮物，是多麼的高興與驚訝！你送的這套美麗的餐具，我們將會長期愛惜。你的愛心，我們言語難以表達。

The lovely blanket you gave our little Lucy is so soft and light that she seems to drop off to sleep when we cover her with it. Bob sends his regards and adds his thanks to mine for your thoughtfulness.

你送給我們小 Lucy 的可愛毯子，既輕便又柔軟，我們蓋在她身上，她很快就睡著了。Bob 附帶向你問好，我們都很感謝你的好意。

(to drop off to sleep＝quickly fall to sleep)

It was most thoughtful and generous of you to send us the handsome bridge set that will play an important part in our married life. It will be a pleasant means of having happy gatherings with friends. Bob joins me in thanking you most heartily for your thoughts of us.

你送給我們漂亮的全套橋牌，真是太窩心，太大方了。這套轎牌在我們婚後的生活中，用途很大，也是朋友歡聚的快樂工具。你的關懷，Bob 與我致上衷心的感謝。

Bob and I most sincerely appreciate the lovely lace tablecloth with napkins. As you know, we both enjoy entertaining friends a great deal. You could not have given us anything better.

Bob 和我實在很欣賞那漂亮有鑲花邊的桌布和餐巾。你知道我們倆位很愛招待朋友，你哪能送給我們比這更好的東西啊！

Your silver candlesticks are perfect as our wedding gift. The design and the contour make them a thing of beauty and a joy forever. Ed joins me in sending you our sincere thanks.

你給我們的銀質蠟燭台作為結婚禮物，實在太棒了。它的設計和形態，成為一種永久的美物和喜悅。Ed 和我致上至誠的謝意。

It seems you have a special talent in selecting gifts people especially desire. That beautiful bedside lamp you gave me not only reminds of my birthday, but also of how much a friend like you means to me.

你似乎有特別天分，能選擇別人想要的禮物。你送我那個漂亮的床頭燈，不但能提醒我的生日，也意味著你這位朋友對我的重要。

Bob and I were overjoyed with the exquisite coffee set. This lovely remembrance of yours will be used and enjoyed constantly with many pleasant thoughts of you. Thank you again very much, Mary.

Bob 和我都很喜歡那套精美的咖啡具。我們會常常使用這個可愛的紀念品，也會懷著美好的心情想念你。Mary，我們再次謝謝你。

How wonderful you were / are to give us such a marvelous set of matched luggage. We will have to take more trips in order to keep it in use.

你送給我們一套特級的相配行李箱，實在太棒了。我們應該多多旅行，才能派上用場。

（it 是指 set）

Thanks seem feeble for such a lovely gift, but we do appreciate it most sincerely.

對這樣漂亮的禮物，謝謝似乎不管用，但我們確是至誠的感激。

I am more than delighted with the tie you sent me for my birthday. You have shown excellent taste in your choice. Many thanks for your thoughtfulness.

你寄給我生日禮物的領帶，我很喜歡。你有很高的挑選品味。非常感謝你的好意。

Our little Lucy is head over heels in love with the lovely doll you sent her. It is so cuddly that she keeps hugging it all day long. No words can fully express my appreciation for your kindness.

我們的小 Lucy，深深愛上你送給她的可愛娃娃。它是那麼逗人喜歡，她整天摟摟抱抱。對你的好意，我們的感激，字眼難以表達。

There is no one on earth more thoughtful and generous than you.
I just don't know how to thank you enough for the beautiful vase
with the Chinese design. It would make any room pretty with fresh
flower in it.

世上沒有人比你更關心更大方。你送我這個有中國式樣的漂亮花
瓶，我不知如何表達足夠的謝意。花瓶插上鮮花時，會使任何房間
顯得美觀。

I was so thrilled today when I opened your package and found a
magnificent gift of steak knife set. Whenever I use this gift, I'll think
of you.

今天當我們打開包裹，看到一套精美的吃牛排刀子，我高興極了。
不論什麼時候使用這套禮物，我都會想到你。

I don't know how to discourage you from sending me such pretty
gifts each year for my birthday.
I deeply appreciate the dessert plates you gave me. They are too
beautiful to use except on special occasions.

我不曉得怎樣阻止你每年送我漂亮的生日禮物。我深深感謝你送我
精美的甜點盤子。太漂亮了，我都捨不得用，只用在特別場合。

Your necklace and earring set was one of the most beautiful gifts I
have received. I was so overwhelmed that it almost brought tears
to my eyes.

你贈送的全套項鍊和耳環，是我收到最漂亮的禮物之一。我太興奮
了，幾乎流出眼淚。

You have certainly kept up your reputation for generosity and good taste in (wedding) anniversary gifts.
Nothing could have pleased Bob and me more than your pretty silver dinner service. We shall be proud to use your gift on many occasions.

你對(結婚)周年禮物的大方和高品味，仍享有聲譽。沒有任何東西比你送給我和 Bob 那套漂亮的銀質餐具更好。我們將在許多場合中得意地使用你的禮物。

(silver dinner service 也叫 silver service set)

How can I ever thank you, Bob, for this glamorous gift, in your excellent taste. Your thinking of me in such a friendly fashion will get off my new year to the very best possible start.

Bob，我真不曉得怎樣謝謝你送我這份高品味美麗動人的禮物。你這種友善的方式關心我，是我最好新年的開始。

(to get off＝to start)

The European vase with pretty pattern you gave me for my retirement is the most beautiful and useful gift I have received. It is going to be much in evidence in my new home. You must come to see how ideally your gift fits into its surroundings here.

你送給我退休的美麗圖樣歐式花瓶，是我收到禮物中最漂亮最有用的。它放在我新房容易見到的地方。你該來看看，你的禮物是多麼適合房間的周圍。

(in evidence 意思是 easily seen)

Ed and I are very grateful for the toaster you gave us. It fills a real need and it is the right size for our kitchen counter. We'll cherish your gift always.

Ed 和我非常感謝你送給我們的烤麵包機，這真符合我們的需求，其大小也適合廚房的檯面。我們會時常珍惜你的禮物。

Thank you so much for the beautiful clock with the lovely inscription. You certainly should not have done this, but it is so typical of your kindness and your thoughtfulness. I will treasure it all my life.

非常謝謝你送我那漂亮並有刻字的時鐘。你實在不要這麼客氣，但這又是你關心和熱誠的獨特表現。我會一輩子珍惜它。

The little pink dress you gave at my baby shower is certainly gorgeous. It is so beautifully made with lace and embroidery. You were so sweet to have gone to all the trouble to buy it. My deep gratitude is endless.

在我的嬰兒禮物會上，你送的粉紅色小套裝，實在太棒了。上面的飾邊和刺繡很漂亮，你費神去選購，很窩心。我有無限的感激。

(baby shower 或 bridal shower 所送的禮物，不能代替結婚禮物或生孩子的禮物)

The check you sent me literally took my breath away. By using it, I can get some special fittings or furniture for my bedroom. Thank you from the bottom of my heart.

你寄給我支票，實在讓我太驚訝了。我可用這張支票，買些我臥房的特別裝備或傢具。我衷心的感謝你。

(to take someone's breath away＝to take away someone's breath，使某人激動或萬分驚訝)

You could not have given me a more suitable gift than the check. I know exactly what I shall do with it. I have been thinking about purchasing a new computer and your check will just get me over the top. You can see now why I am so grateful to you.

你送我的禮物，沒有比支票更合適，我知道怎樣使用它。我一直想要買個新電腦，你的支票正可派上用場。現在你知道我為何這麼感激你。

Thank you so much for the graduation check. I knew right away what I was going to do with it. I have been needing and wanting a digital camera for a long time. When I use it, every time I will think of you with affection and gratitude.

非常謝謝你贈送的畢業支票禮物，我馬上知道怎樣使用它 。我很久就想買個數位照相機。以後每當使用時，我會以至誠的感激想到你。

（老外現在也贈送支票禮物，認為很實惠）

To me, the expression, "You should not have done that" seems to be worn-out. I am almost accustomed to your generosity. All members of my family enjoy your gift of a beautiful Chinese painting. Please accept our sincere thanks for your kindness.

「你不要這麼客氣」這句話，對我來說，已經失去作用。你的慷慨，我也習慣了。我家人都喜愛你送的那幅美麗的中國畫。你的愛心，請接受我至誠的謝意。

I was happy enough to hear from you at the Holiday season, let alone receiving a gift from you. The exquisite necklace you sent me really matches my new dress. Thanks for the gift and the lovely Christmas card.

在(聖誕)假期中,能有你的消息,我真是太高興了,更不用說,收到你的禮物。你寄來的精美項鍊,非常配稱我的新衣。謝謝你的禮物和聖誕賀卡。

(Holiday season 通常是指聖誕季節)

Your presence meant a great deal to us and your unexpected gift delighted us all. I'll cherish your beautiful vase and whenever I look at it, it will always remind me of you.

你能出席參加,對我們很夠意思。沒想到你還送禮,更使我們高興。我會珍惜你的漂亮花瓶。每當我看到它,我都會想起你。

 ## 謝招待(Thank for hospitality)

例如:

Last weekend's luncheon with you and Bob was a real treat long to be remembered. It was a pleasure to see how happy and healthy you both are. I hope some day I may have an opportunity to return your kindness.

上周末與你和 Bob 共進午餐,真是一次長久回憶的盛舉。看到你們兩位健康快樂,令人欣慰。盼望有一天,我也有機會回報你的愛心。

Thank you for being such a wonderful hostess. You always make certain I am comfortable, wellfed and welcome. No words of mine can compliment you too highly.

謝謝你這位一級棒的女主人。你總是讓我感到舒適，吃得好和受到歡迎。我沒有字眼能好好誇獎你。

We ate too much and stayed too late because we were entertained by the most wonderful host and hostess in town. Our compliments to the chef!

我們吃太多了，也逗留太久了，因為我們受到城內最棒男女主人的招待。我們向主廚致敬。

What a delightful dinner party! We have always enjoyed going to your home, but last Saturday's visit was more delightful than ever.

那是多麼愉快的宴會！我們一向喜歡到府上，但是上星期六的拜訪，比過去更愉快。

It was a real treat to have spent a weekend with you. We enjoyed every minute of it and can't get over the delicious meals we had. We'll not expect to forget such a joyful experience for some time.

能與你們共度周末，實在太棒了。我們享受到每分鐘的愉快。那些美味的餐點，更難忘懷。這種美好經驗，許久不會忘記。

The Sunday night get-together was just great, and the companionship throughout the entire evening was particularly enjoyable. Thanks again for your gracious hospitality.

星期天晚上的團聚，真是太好了，尤其整晚的友好氣氛，更是令人愉快。再次謝謝你的殷勤招待。

The dinner party at your home last Saturday was a real delight for which no words can express my appreciation. Your delicious food and the pleasant talk afterward have left such a warm glow in me that I almost forgot the strenuous week of my work.

上星期六在府上的宴會，實在太高興了，無法表達我的感謝。你們美味的食物和會後的聊天，也留給我熱情的喜悅。我幾乎忘了一星期緊張的工作。

It is a double pleasure to send my gratitude for your charming hospitality at your dancing party. I really appreciate such gracious entertainment! I will recall such a delightful evening often. Again thank you most sincerely.

在你的舞會上，你的美好招待，我深深地感謝。我很欣賞那種高雅的款待。我常常會回憶這次愉快的晚上。再度誠懇地謝謝你。

We are still talking about the wonderful weekend we spent with you. Even if you are the busiest people in town, you still welcome us into your home as if nothing in the world were more important.

我們還在談論與你共度周末的事。即使你是市內最忙的人物，你還是歡迎我們到府上，好像世上沒有比這更重要的事。

Your asking me to dinner last Sunday was my most pleasant time in ages. With much work to do and little time, I realized how stimulating it was to relax and enjoy our conversation and friendship. It was the lift and the change I needed. I send my hearty gratitude to you.

上周日你請我吃飯，是我長久以來最愉快的時刻。我工作忙碌，少有時間，體會到與你聊天和友誼，是多麼的輕鬆愉快。這也是我需要振奮和轉換的時刻。我致上衷心的感謝。

We'll think of your warm hospitality with gratitude and pleasure for a long time to come. Thank you for the absolutely perfect weekend.

我們將以感激和愉快的心情長久記得你熱情的招待。那確是一個完美的周末。謝謝你。

The barbecue in your backyard last Sunday will long be remembered. The relaxed atmosphere and the casual dress were a treat for us. I apprectiate your hospitality more than I can say.

上周日在府上後院的烤肉餐，將會讓人長久的回憶。那種輕鬆的氣氛，和隨意的服裝，對我們來說，也是一種樂趣。我對於你招待的感謝之情，無法言諭。

The dinner party was lovely and I was delighted to be included. I don't know anyone who has as much flair and style as you do when it comes to entertaining.

那次餐宴太好了，我很高興被邀請參加。談到請客招待，我不知道還有誰能比你更有才華和氣派。

Many, many thanks to both of you for a lovely evening of (playing) bridge. It was a great pleasure to spend some time with you. How sweet / dear / kind / thoughtful of you to remember me / think of me.

多謝你們兩位，我有個愉快打橋牌的晚上，能與你們在一起是十分高興的事。你們能記得我，是多麼窩心啊！

Your courtesy and hospitality to me and my daughter during our visit in New York was something we shall never forget. You certainly added greatly to the pleasure of our stay in the city. Although she has written you her thanks, I wanted to add my own.

我們在紐約作客時，你對我和小女的好意與招待，使我們永不忘記。你的確大大增加了我們在該市停留的愉快心情，雖然她已去信向你致謝，但我也要加上我的謝意。

Not only were you diligent, but you were friendly and kind as well. Thanks for making our trip to your city a memorable one. Lilly and I really enjoyed the time you spent with us. We both appreciate your faithful friendship.

你不但細緻勤奮，也很友愛貼心。謝謝你使我們前往你們城市，成為一次值得回憶的旅行。能與你們在一起，Lilly 和我都很愉快，我們也感佩你這種真誠的友誼。

Thank you to everyone for the warm and generous welcome on Saturday night. We really appreciated everyone's kindness and good spirits. Seeing you all again was simply wonderful.

謝謝每一位為星期六晚上親切和熱烈的歡迎。我們的確欣賞每一位的善意和活力。能再度見到你們太棒了。

A special thank to Bob and Mary for opening their beautiful home and bringing us all together. We look forward to future gatherings.

特別感謝 Bob 和 Mary，開放他們漂亮的房子，供我們歡聚一堂。我們期待將來再有這樣的歡聚。

謝幫忙（Thanks for assistance or help）

包括朋友為你補習英語，籌備基金，寫推薦信，開派對或其他不同的協助與支持。

例如：

Your teaching English as a volunteer has provided another avenue to help many Chinese immigrants achieve their potential. We don't know how to express our gratitude, but we hope you know how we feel.

你為許多中國移民擔任義工、講授英語，是提供他們達到潛力的另一種途徑。我們不知如何表達我們的感謝，但我們希望你能了解我們內心的感受。

（avenue＝way）

It's hard to put into words my hearty appreciation for your helpfulness in smoothing out the roughness of my thesis. Without your assistance, I would not have graduated from this prestigious university.

你幫我把粗略草率的論文，洗鍊成清晰流暢，我對你的感激，言語難以表達。要不是因為你的幫忙，我也許不能從這所名大學畢業。

Many thanks for all the assistance, information and encouragement you offered us when our son was applying to Stanford University. We also appreciate your kind expression of congratulations when he was accepted (by Stanford).

當我們的兒子申請史丹福大學時，非常感謝你給我們所有的幫忙、訊息和鼓勵。我們也謝謝你對他能進史大的親切祝賀。

Thanks a million for your mentoring my English learning over the years. I have never found you to be at a loss for an answer concerning colloquialisms or slang. Your knowledge of the English language is seemingly encyclopedic.

感謝你多年來指導我的英語學習，在俚語或口語方面，你從來沒有不能回答的問題。你的英語知識，似乎太淵博了。

A big thank for taking care of our son Bob during his studies in the U.S. We will be most grateful if you continue to help him and steer him in the right direction.

謝謝你照顧我們在美讀書的兒子。你如能繼續幫他，引導他走向正確方向，我們將會銘感至內。

How wonderful it is to have someone like you to be a volunteer interpreter whenever we need one particularly for medical cases. Your kind assistance to me and my family members in solving our language barrier will always be appreciated and remembered.

不管什麼時候，我們能有一位像你這樣的義務翻譯，尤其是看病，實在太棒了。你幫我和我家人解決語言困難，時時受到感激和銘記在心。

Your continued encouragement and support in my writing for the newspaper have given me an attitude of thankfulness and a sense of gratefulness.

你為我在報上寫稿而繼續鼓勵和支持，使我既感謝又感恩。

We both wish to express our appreciation for the time and trouble you took caring for the house and the yard when we were in Taiwan. We feel blessed to have such loving and faithful neighbor / friend.

我們回台灣時，你們費時費神照顧我們的房子和庭院，我們要向你致謝。我們有這樣友愛和忠誠的鄰居／朋友，實在太有福氣了。

Thank you for the fine care you have consistently delivered to my parents over the years. I hope you know how much you are appreciated today and every day.

謝謝你多年來對我父母不斷的細心照顧，希望你知道我們天天都在感激。

I want to thank you from the bottom of my heart for your incredible assistance over the last five years. I am moving on to the next chapter of my career, but I'll never forget the support that you gave me.

過去五年來，你對我極度的協助，我衷心的感謝。現在我進入事業另一章節，但我永不忘記你給我的支持。

Working as a volunteer, you have been pushing the limits to help us. You are like our right hand, for which we are very grateful.

你擔任義工，超出範圍地幫助我們，你真是我們的得力助手，我們非常感激。

（這裡用 limit，而不用 limitation，以免被人誤為 handicapped）

On behalf of my family members, I want to thank you for the splendid job you did arranging our anniversary event. It was an outstanding success in every way.

你為我們的(結婚)紀念日籌備慶典，你辦得太棒了，在各方面，都稱一流。我代表家人向你致謝。

The letter of recommendation you so kindly wrote for me must have been terrific. I was called yesterday with a job offer. I am grateful beyond words for all the support you have given me.

你這麼好意為我寫推薦信，一定寫得很棒，昨天我獲得工作的通知。你給我支持，我內心的感激字眼難以表達。

It is my understanding that you wrote a letter supporting my nomination as an Outstanding Faculty of the Year. I was so glad to have been honored with this title. I am deeply appreciative of your kind support (in this regard).

我知道你寫了一封信，支持提名我為「年度優良教師」，我很高興已經獲得這個頭銜。你的支持，我深為感謝。

Over the years, I have been very grateful to you for mentoring me in learning my second language. Your profound knowledge of English has helped me improve both my reading and writing. Again, thanks for all that I have learned from you.

我很感謝你多年來指導我學習第二語文，你的淵博英文知識，使我在閱讀和寫作方面得到進步。再次謝謝，我從你那兒學到不少東西。

Having asked you to keep an eye on my house during my one-month absence, I thank you for going above and beyond the call of duty in patrolling our neighborhood. We are so fortunate to have a police officer like you.

我要求你在我外出一個月期間，請你注意一下我的房子。我謝謝你超過工作範圍在我們鄰近巡邏。我們有像你這樣的警官，太幸運了。

(to go above and beyond＝to do more)

Just a hasty note to thank you for your complimentary mention of my books in your article in last Sunday's newspaper. Earning your favorable evaluation makes me as happy as my publisher will be.

我只是匆匆寫這封短信，謝謝你在上周日報紙上所刊登的大作中，誇獎我的書。能得到你的好評估，使我和我的出版公司同樣開心。

During the time of my difficulties, your selflessness, thoughtfulness and kind assistance show me a whole new world of loving, giving and fun. You have made my life brighter and more meaningful.

在我困難的時候，你的無私奉獻，考慮周到和親切幫忙，給我感到一種富於愛心、互助和快樂的新世界。你使我的生活更光明，更有意義。

I am grateful to you for co-hosting a luncheon for the Chinese delegation. You have taken much of the pressure of planning the event off my shoulders.

謝謝你共同接待中國代表團。你為我籌劃這件事，分擔了許多的壓力。

Having a baby shower for me was such a thrill that I don't know how to thank you adequately for your kindness and thoughtfulness.

你為我舉辦一項嬰兒送禮會，實在是件令人興奮的事。我不知如何謝謝你的好意和關心才好。

(baby shower 或 bridal shower 都由好友主辦，不能由自己的媽媽或姐妹主辦)

My wife and I appreciate so much your helping us during our financial hardship. Your reaching-out and pitching-in will always be remembered.

內人和我十分感謝你在我們經濟困難時的幫助。你伸出援手，作出奉獻，我們會常常記得。

With a big heart, you always have the initiative to do what you can to help whenever you see me with a problem. I have never seen anyone more devoted to helping others. I am lucky to have you as a friend.

由於你的心地善良，你只要看到我有問題，你就主動地幫助我。我從未見過任何人如此幫助他人。我有你這樣的朋友，真是幸運。

Thank you for your contribution of $500 to the Flood Relief Fund. Your gift will be used where most needed.
Your generosity and kindness will help those victims to have a temporary place to live.

謝謝你為水災救援基金捐款五百元。你的禮物將會按需要的地方，善加利用。你的慷慨和愛心，將幫助那些災民有個暫時的住所。

It is good to know that whether the needy face poverty, hunger, anguish or other challenges, you are always there to support their physical and spiritual needs.

很高興知道不論那些貧困者面臨窮苦、飢餓、悲痛或其他的挑戰，你都會支持他們身體上和精神上的需求。

(the needy 指需要幫助的貧困者)

To you, I can never fully convey in words my hearty appreciation for everything you have done for me.
I thank you for the important role you have played in my life.

你為我所做所為，我無法以字眼充分表達內心的感激。謝謝你在我人生中，扮演了重要的角色。

Your financial support enables us to continue offering the less fortunate in our area the strength and protection they need. We are indebted (或 very much obliged) to you for what you have done for us.

你的經濟支援，使我們能繼續供給我們地區貧困者所需的力量和保護。我們深深感謝你為我們所做的一切。

(the less fortunate = the needy)

Thank you so much for agreeing to speak on U.S. China relations in our school. We are very much looking forward to hearing your presentation. I believe the audience will enjoy your expertise on the subject.

謝謝你願意光臨本校，談論中美關係，我們期待恭聽你的高見。我相信聽眾會欣賞你對主題的專長。

Over the past years, your cooperation and perseverance in my project have been highly helpful. I thank you profusely for having been the kind of friend I can count on.

過去多年來，你對我方案的合作和堅持，受益不淺。我非常感謝有這麼一位可靠的朋友。

As a Principal, I would like to express my gratitude for donating a $10,000 scholarship for needy students. Your attitude of caring and sharing will help dispel the epidemic of greed and self-interest that has permeated our society today.

身為校長，我要謝謝你捐獻一萬元作為貧困學生的獎學金。你的關懷與分享，有助消除目前充滿社會的貪婪和利己的通病。

I am extremely grateful to everyone who put forth the time and effort, as well as those who donated money for my long-term project.

你們每位為了我的長期方案，付出時間和力量，以及那些人的捐款，我非常的感激。

（to put forth＝to give）

We are so grateful for what you did for us even with your busy schedule, but you have never gained a nickel from helping others. You really have brought hope to the hopeless.

我們感謝你在百忙中幫助我們，但你幫助他人，從不求回報，你真為那些絕望者帶來希望。

(to gain a nickel＝to gain a penny＝to benefit)

As a scholar, you are known for your vast knowledge of the English language. You have touched the lives of nearly every Chinese student in our school. We want to express our appreciation for your professional assistance.

身為一位學者，你的廣博英語知識，人人皆知。你在本校幾乎感動每位中國學生。你的專業性幫助，我們甚表感謝。

We all owe a debt of gratitude to you for caring about less fortunate children throughout our community. Your donation, warmth and sincerity make them feel important, needed and appreciated.

你為我們社區照顧那些貧困的孩子，我們尤其感謝你的捐獻，熱心和至誠，使他們覺得自己重要，受到幫助和重視。

Your fundraising efforts in establishing a scholarship for needy students have been overwhelming. The generosity shown by your employees is nothing short of amazing. Thanks from the bottom of our hearts.

你為了貧困學生籌募獎學金的努力，是極大的成功；你們員工的慷慨表現，令人驚異。我們衷心的感謝。

(nothing short of amazing＝really amazing＝fully amazing)

Thank you for my salary increase which is always welcome from a monetary point of view. It assures me that I am performing my job in a satisfactory fashion. Again, my sincere thanks.

謝謝你為我加薪，站在金錢方面來說，很受歡迎。這也使我放心，我的工作表現處於滿意情況。再次向你致至誠的感謝。

In appreciation for your hard work and dedication, you will be given an extra two percent merit pay increase starting January the first, 2012.

為了謝謝你的工作努力和獻身精神，自 2012 年元月一日起，你將取得另外 2% 工作優良獎勵的加薪。

No suitable words can fully express my gratitude for helping me solve so many problems. You handled the situations with proficiency, humanity and professionalism.

你幫我解決許多問題，我沒有適當的字眼能充分表達我的感激。你處理情況都是那麼熟練，有人性和專業精神。

Your dedication to providing uplifting and heart-warming programs to enhance the lives of critically ill people is greatly appreciated by all of us. Your help in this regard was phenomenal.

你為那些嚴重病患，提供振奮窩心的活動，提高了他們的生命力。你的奉獻精神，我們十分感激。你在這方面的幫助，是一級棒。

Through your generous financial support, we have been able to take on this ambitious project. We appreciate the efforts you have made to meet specific requests and needs.

由於你慷慨的經濟支援，我們才能開始這個雄心的計畫。我們感謝你為了配合特別的需求而作出努力。

(to take on＝to begin)

Just a quick note to compliment you most sincerely on the outstanding performance you made this year. It is only through devotion and persistence that such an accomplishment can come about.

只是寫幾個字，至誠地稱讚你今年工作的特佳表現。這種成就，只有從奉獻和毅力，才能達到。

(to come about＝to achieve or to happen)

I don't want to be unappreciative when you have done so much for our department. Thanks a million, Bob, for doing such an excellent job.

你為我們部門做了這麼多事，我不能不領情。Bob，非常感謝你做得這麼出色。

You have done so many wonderful things that let others see God's goodness and love shining through. This thank-you is really a prayer that His blessings will shine upon you.

你做了許多了不起的事，讓別人看到上帝的慈愛發出光亮。這封謝函，算是一種禱告，願上帝的恩典，也在你身上發光。

When I asked you how I could repay you for your assistance, you replied, "Just do the same for someone else." I will gladly pass the favor forward, but my deep gratitude is endless.

當我問你我要如何報答你的幫助，你回答：「只要照樣幫助別人就好。」我會高興地將你的好意推動，但我還是無限的感激。

Your motto, "I never expect anything from anyone" makes me reluctant to send you anything. But I still want you to know how much I am grateful for what you have done for me.

你的座右銘「我從不期待任何人的任何回報」使我不敢寄給你任何東西。但我仍要你知道，我是多麼感激你為我所做的一切。

Your generosity and willingness to serve others merit our recognition and praise because the true measure of an individual is found in the way he / she treats people.

你的慷慨和樂意服務他人，值得我們的賞識和表揚。因為真正衡量一個人，就是從他(她)對待他人的方式，可以看出。

I want to thank you for all the time you put into helping me for my research project. I hope I can in some way return the favor.

謝謝你為我的研究計畫，花了許多時間。盼望我能對你的恩惠有所報答。

You have helped them open their eyes to the possibilities of the world around them. Your generosity has given those in need the opportunities of a lifetime.

你已經幫助他們對世界周圍的可能性打開眼界：你的慷慨資助，也給那些貧困者一生許多機會。

Many thanks for not only spreading the word to those around you, but also for helping us do the most good for struggling men, women and families here in our community. Many of them simply need a hand with the basics.

非常感謝你向周圍的人傳播訊息，也為我們社區那些為生活掙扎的男女和家庭做出最好的幫助。其實他們許多人僅僅只要基本生活需求。

(need a hand＝need help)

Your kind assistance for those who live on the edge of desperation is a wonderful goal to which you are committed.

你親切地幫助那些生活在失望的邊緣者 ，是你承諾的一個偉大目標。

We are thankful to know that we can count on you as we continue to battle against the harsh realities faced the helpless in our community.

我們能繼續為社區那些無助者的嚴酷現實問題而搏鬥：我們還能靠你的支持，甚為感激。

 ## 謝慰問（Thanks for sympathy）

例如：

We appreciate your very kind message of sympathy at the loss of our father. His passing was a blow from which it will take a long time to recover.

我們感謝你對家父去逝的親切慰問。他的離開，是個震驚，需要一段長時間才能恢復過來。

I can't begin to tell you how much your message of sympathy meant to me in my sorrow. It helps tremendously to know that I have such devoted friends to comfort me.

在我悲傷時刻，你的安慰話語，對我發生的作用程度，很難向你道出。我有如此忠誠的朋友安慰我，是種極大的扶持。

Many thanks to you for your concerns and kind messages during my mother's long illness. Everyone in my family cherishes your wonderful friendship.

非常感謝你對家母長期生病的關懷和親切問候。我們家人每一位都很珍惜你的偉大友誼。

Your kind note at the time of bereavement makes my burden a little lighter. Your beautiful tribute to my father was greatly appreciated.

你的親切話語，減輕一些我悲痛時刻的精神負擔。你對先父的讚揚，至為感謝。

(tribute＝praise)

Thank you for helping Bob look forward to bright and promising tomorrows. Your words of comfort and kindness meant a great deal to us during his illness.

謝謝你幫助 Bob 期盼著光明美好的明天。在他生病中，你的安慰和關愛，對我們也是意味深長。

Your kind assistance and cheerful messages did much to keep him from being bored to extinction during his illness. It is really a blessing to have a friend like you.

你親切的協助和振奮的訊息，使他在生病中不至悶得要死。有你這樣的朋友，真是上帝的賜福。

The kindness and generosity you showed at the time of my father's passing are much appreciated. We are very blessed to count you as a friend.

非常感謝你在先父去逝時所表達的關懷和愛心。我們很感恩能有你這樣的朋友。

You may not know how much it meant to me when I received your beautiful fresh flower. I feel, in a very real way, your love, strength, and support during my illness.

當我收到你漂亮鮮花時，你不曉得那對我意義多麼深厚。在我生病中，我真正感受到你給我的關愛、力量和支持。

Thank you so much for your kind expression of condolence. It is wonderful to know that I have so many friends who share my sorrow.

謝謝你親切的慰問。我有這麼多朋友分擔我的悲傷，實在太好了。

A thank-you to you and your staff members who have inquired about my health and sent best wishes. I am so grateful that there are people in our community to be counted on.

謝謝你和你的同仁探問有關我的健康和祝福。我很感激我能指望我們社區這些人。

Your unconditional love and bottomless support during my sad time will never be forgotten. With your optimistic and witty attitude, you cheer me in my season of gloom and encourage me to look forward with great faith to a bright future.

在我難過時，你無條件的關愛和無限的支持，令我難以忘懷。在我沮喪時，你的樂觀和風趣態度，使我振奮，並且鼓勵我懷著信心走向光明的未來。

（這裡的 season＝time）

注意事項：

(1)只要別人為你花時間，費精力或花錢等，通常老外都會寄謝卡。（Thank-you note is a must whenever someone has gone out of their way to do something nice for you.）

(2)謝卡不是長信，通常很簡短扼要 ，即是卡片上印有感謝字樣，也要親筆寫上幾個字，表示親切。（Thank-you

note does not have to be long and flowery. Short and to-the-point can be more effective.）

(3)謝卡最好早寄，但遲寄總比不寄好。（A late note of thanks is better than no thanks at all.）

Chapter 5

老美怎樣寫推薦信

在美國要想找個白領工作（多半是專業或半專業性）或進入高等學府深造，似乎都要推薦信（letter of recommendation/reference），不論為學生、同事、部屬或朋友寫，都是一件「花時間」、「傷腦筋」的差事。難怪也有老中乾脆說：「你自己寫，我簽名就行。」

的確，在這工作繁忙，生活緊張的社會裡，大家都在追求辦事簡單、快速與方便。於是我就想出這種「偷懶」省時的辦法，把一般專業性與半專業性推薦信內容，大致分為：(1)開頭語(2)品德修養(3)學歷與經驗(4)工作表現(5)結尾語。（老外特別重視品德修養和工作能力，所以例句較多）。

需要時，由各項例句中，挑選一些想要而適合的句子，再把句中的人名、職位和機構的名稱，加以改變，只要段落分明，就可組成一封推薦信。希望這對一些老中，有點幫助（至少是 guideline）。

開頭語（Introduction）

通常包括寫信的目的，與被推薦者的關係或申請工作的性質等。(信中第一次提起被推薦者，要寫其全名)。

例如：

It is a pleasure to write a letter of recommendation on behalf of Mr. Chung-hua Lee who has applied to you for a computer programming position.

能為李中華先生申請電腦程式工作寫封推薦信，是件愉快的事。

At the request of Mr. Robert Smith, a former student of mine, I am writing this letter in support of his application.

我以前的一位學生 Robert Smith，要我為他寫這封信支持他的申請。

Miss Fu-mei Lin has worked as a graduate student under my direction from May 2, 2007 to date. She has asked me to write on her behalf and I willingly offer the following comments:

從 2007 年 5 月 2 日到現在，林富美小姐在我指導下，擔任研究生工作。她要我為她寫這封信，我很願意提出以下觀點：

This is to recommend Jack Wang who comes from a family of good standing in Taiwan.

在此推薦 Jack 王先生，他係來自台灣名聲良好的家庭。

Mr. Chung-hua Lee entered National Taiwan University in 2001 and received his B.S. in engineering in 2004. During that time he was a student in my class.

李中華先生在 2001 年進入台大，2004 年取得工程學士，那時他是我班上的學生。

Mr. Robert Smith began as a research assistant in 2005 and was promoted through several increasingly responsible positions until he reached his present position as a senior research fellow.

2005 年 Robert Smith 先生開始只是一名研究助理，經過數次晉升後，才達到目前資深研究員的職位。

I am pleased to have the opportunity of providing a reference for Mr. Robert Wang.

我很高興有機會為 Robert 王先生提供一封推薦信。

Miss Mary Chen worked in my department as an accounting assistant for five years. She was responsible for preparation of financial reports such as balance sheets and profit and loss statements.

Mary 陳小姐在本部門擔任會計助理五年。她負責準備財務報告，諸如決算表和損益報表。

I understand that Mr. Chung-hua Lee is being considered for a computer position in your company. I truly believe that you will find him to be an excellent employee.

我知道貴公司正在考慮李中華先生所申請的電腦工作，我深信您會發現他是一位優秀的員工。

Mr. Edward Wang has been my faithful friend and working associate for ten years. I am pleased to have this opportunity to commend on his many contributions.

Edward 王先生是我十年來忠誠的朋友和工作的伙伴。我很高興有機會讚賞他許多的貢獻。

For more than ten years I have known Mr. Robert Wang and his family. He comes from a Christian family refined and highly respected in our community.

我認識 Robert 王先生和他的家人已經十多年了，他來自有教養的基督教家庭，在我們社區裡高度受人尊敬。

Over the last five years, my association with Mr. Bob Li has enabled me to observe him closely. I am more than happy to recommend him as a fine man healthy in mind and body.

我與 Bob 李先生過去五年來的交往，使我能接近了解他。我很高興推薦他是位身心健全的男士。

Miss Mary Chen has asked me to write you in regard to her experience and abilities as a math teacher. She possesses traits which permit me to recommend her to you without hesitation.

Mary 陳小姐要我寫這封信給您，有關她擔任數學教師的經驗和能力。她所具備的特點使我毫不猶豫地向您推薦。

Mr. James Lin was my student from 2001-2004, during which time I was serving as associate professor. Throughout the years he was consistently involved with curricular activities.

從 2001 年到 2004 年 James 林先生是我的學生，那時我是副教授。在那些年，他常常參加課業方面的活動。

This is to certify that I was a colleague of Bob Wang when we both were on the faculty of James College, and that I know him well.

茲證明當我和 Bob 王先生在 James 大學教書時，他是我的同事，並且我對他很熟悉。

I have known Miss Mary Li since she came to this university as a freshman participating in our honors program, I have also had the pleasure of teaching her and working with her in school activities.

自從 Mary 李小姐來到本大學參加我們大一新生榮譽課程時，我就認識她。我很高興能教到她而且與她一同辦理學校活動。

Mr. Chung-hua Li has been very closely associated with me for the past five years. When he leaves our department as of the first of next month, we will miss him.

過去五年來，李中華先生與我共事密切，下月一號起，他將離開我們單位，我們會很想念他。

As a lab assistant with this department, Mr. Robert Chen has worked under my supervision for the past three years. He has been completely reliable and kept the lab in excellent condition.

Robert 王先生在我指導下，做了三年的實驗室助理。他十分可靠，並且把實驗室保持得井井有條。

Mr. Robert Smith has asked that I write a letter of reference based on our professional connection during the past five years.

Robert Smith 先生請我寫這封推薦信是根據我們過去五年來專業上的來往。

品德修養（Personality and character）

一般包括誠實可靠，為人相處和熱心服務等。（這些都是老外特別重視的，他們對學位和名校反而列為次要）

例如：

Miss A is a congenial, pleasant and intelligent young lady. With her pleasing personality, she gets along unusually well with her fellow staff members.

A 小姐是位和藹親切，才智聰慧的姑娘；她有令人喜愛的個性，與同事相處得特別和諧。

He respects others and treats them with dignity. The time I spent with Mr. A was an illuminating and rewarding one.

A 先生以尊重的態度敬愛他人。我與他相處，可謂獲益不淺，也是極有意義的時光。

His sense of humor has made life happier and easier for those who know him. He is honest with people, dedicated to his job and loyal to his friends.

他的幽默感使周圍認識他的人感到生活更愉快與安閒。他對人誠實，獻身於工作，對朋友也是忠心耿耿。

Mr. B is a very likeable and personable gentleman. His initiative and willingness to take responsibility has been impressive.

B 先生是位討人喜歡的翩翩紳士，他那積極性的負責意願，令人印象深刻。

Highly regarded by his colleagues for a pleasant and conscientious manner, Mr. A was our team leader and a sincere, hardworking and dependable employee.

A 先生的和藹和認真態度，受到他同仁的高度評價。他是我們團隊的主力，也是誠懇、努力、可靠的員工。

Miss A is considered by our staff as a warm, kind-hearted individual who was well-liked and respected by her co-workers.

A 小姐被我們同仁認為是位熱誠，富愛心的人，她也受到同事們的喜愛和尊敬。

It was my privilege to enjoy his friendship. I have found him a delightful and personable person, whose first thought seems to be "What can I do for you?"

我很榮幸能享受到他的友誼。我發現他是位討人喜愛的人，他的第一個念頭似乎就是「我能為你效勞什麼？」

He has been not only a colleague, but a personal friend as well. I particularly like his pleasant personality and his ability to get along well with others.

他不但是同事，也是私交，尤其我喜歡他那令人愉快的性格，以及與人和睦相處的能力。

I have gained much from the charm, sweetness, personality and wisdom that she has shown upon many occasions. She has been a dedicated staff member.

她在許多場所所表現的魅力，和藹以及性格智慧，使我獲益良多。她在同仁中也是熱誠的一員。

She is very considerate of the feelings of others and always puts them ahead of herself. She is appreciative of even the smallest things that people do for her.

她十分體諒別人的感受，她總是把別人放在首位，即使別人為她做點小事，她都會感激不盡。

Miss A is very modest about her success. After being chosen for the outstanding student award, she never mentioned it to others.

A 小姐對她的成就十分謙遜，當她得到傑出學生獎後，她從未告訴他人。

While very few youngsters give their parents much credit, Miss B likes to tell others how grateful she is to her parents for all they have done for her.

當很少年輕人稱讚他們父母的功勞時，B 小姐總是喜歡告訴別人她對父母為她所做的一切，十分感激。

Her personal charm and attractiveness accompanied by compassion and sincerity enable her to have excellent relations with other colleagues.

她的個人魅力和嫵媚動人，加上愛心和誠懇，使她與其他同仁相處得非常和睦。

You'll enjoy his enthusiastic approach to everything he does. When he is around, somehow everyone seems to function better.

你會喜歡他那副做事的熱心態度，只要他在周圍，大家工作似乎顯得更有勁。

Miss A is a lovely person, attractive with a good sense of humor. I found her to be a sincere and helpful colleague with whom it was a pleasure to work.

A 小姐是位可愛嫵媚動人而富幽默感的人。我發現她對同仁很誠懇，肯助人，與她共事是件愉快的事。

Over the past five years. I have found him to be a young man of high integrity and good character.

過去五年來，我發現他是高度正直，品格良好的青年。

I am privileged to be associated with Mr. A in his social life and feel enriched by his charm, sincerity and warmth.

在社交上，我很慶幸與 A 先生相處。由於他的魅力、真誠和盛情，使我感到充實。

Mr. A was always patient and unfailingly polite. My association with him has been pleasant, professional and productive.

A 先生經常有耐心，一貫很客氣。我與他的交往是愉快的，專業性的，和富有成效的。

After working with him, I became close to Mr. A and came to admire him personally as well as professionally.

我與 A 先生共事後，與他來往密切，同時對他的個性和專業都很敬佩。

Ever since Mr. A has worked here as a researcher, he earned respect from faculty and students. If anyone deserved to brag about accomplishments, it would be he.

自從 A 先生在此擔任研究員以來，他得到教職員和學生的敬愛。假如有人值得誇獎成就的話，應該是他吧！

Mr. Wang is a courteous, intelligent and personable young man who has served this company well in his capacity as a technical researcher.

王先生是位有禮貌，聰明而受人喜歡的青年，他在本公司擔任技術研究員，表現良好。

He is a no-nonsense, fun-loving person and an unconditional friend.

他是位講究實際，十分風趣的人，也是一位無條件的朋友。

If things became difficult or if he caught himself in a mistake, he was likely to strive harder. He created a contagious spirit of cheerfulness among us.

如果事情遭到困難，或是他犯了錯，他可能更加努力。在我們之中，他製造一種有感染性的愉快氣氛。

Wherever Mr. A goes, he draws responses of respect, admiration and affection. Rarely does anyone come to know him without being grateful for the privilege.

不管 A 先生到哪裡，他都會受到尊敬和愛慕。認識他的人，很少不感恩榮幸。

He is a quiet, industrious and careful worker, with above-average concern for detail and accuracy. He perfers to work independently with self-confidence.

他是位沉默、勤奮和細心的員工，對細節和精確也很注意；他很有自信，喜歡獨立工作。

I have frequently heard people praising Mr. A, but never heard an unkind remark about him.

我常常聽到人們誇獎 A 先生，從未聽到對他不好的評語。

His understanding of human nature, his interest in school life and his friendliness to others endear him to students and faculty.

他對人性的了解，對學校生活的興趣，以及對他人的友善，使他受到師生的喜愛。

During his association with our school, Mr. A has gained the respect of students and faculty by his vigorous and broad-minded attitude and by his willingness to set aside his own opinions to consider others' view points.

A 先生在本校工作以來，得到師生的尊敬，因為他有充沛的活力，和開闊的心胸。他願意拋開自己的意見，去考慮別人的看法。

He has brought to every decision a sense of fairness. His human compassion and respect for others endear him to many.

他對每個決定都有公平性；他對人性的同情和尊重，使許多人喜歡他。

His common sense, warm personality and kindness have made him a popular and effective teacher.

他的常識，熱情的性格，以及和藹可親，使他成為一位廣受歡迎、工作效率不錯的教師。

Mr. A was a good organizer and a pleasant young man, efficient, sincere and unassuming, incapable of putting on airs.

A 先生是位很有條理和令人喜歡的青年；他做事有效率、誠懇、不裝腔作勢，也不會擺架子。

He is distinctly above average in emotional control and stability. He is typically optimistic, enthusiastic and cheerful.

他在情緒上的控制和穩定，明顯地高過一般人；他是典型的樂觀、熱心和喜悅。

Mr. B combined the qualities of good sense, absence of conceit and warm humanity. His consideration and thoughtfulness to those who work in this company have earned their respect and affection.

B 先生將良好的判斷力、不自高自大、仁慈博愛集於一身。他對本公司同仁的關懷與體貼，贏得尊敬和愛戴。

Working with Mr. A was one of the most rewarding experiences I have had. He was not only my colleague but my friend. His sense of humor has always been a huge part on our working relationship.

與 A 先生共事，是我最有意義的經驗之一；他不但是我的同事，也是我的朋友。他的幽默感是我們工作關係的一大部分。

I am (was) constantly impressed with his ability to develop rapport with both staff members and professional colleagues.

他與專業同仁和職員們建立良好關係的能力，常常讓我留下深刻的印象。

Miss A has unquestionable character, very high moral standards and excellent conduct at all times.

A 小姐具有無可置疑的品德，高度的倫理水平，並且一向行為良好。

No matter how much he has accomplished, Mr. A always remains very humble, unselfish and unspoiled.

不論 A 先生有多少的成就，他總是十分謙虛，不謀私利，也不損壞原有的品格。

He is also a good follower and willingly supports others in leadership roles. He is unusually happy and supportive in the successes of his peers.

他也是一位很好的追隨者，願意擁護他人的領導。他對同仁的成就，異常的高興和支持。

Mr. Wang has a particularly easygoing and adaptable manner which makes him pleasant to work with. His intelligence always allows him to grasp situations in good perspective.

王先生態度尤其隨和，隨機應變，使同仁樂於與他共事。他的才智，使他能用合理方法掌握情況。

I have known Mr. A for the past twenty years, and can vouch for his character and personality.

我認識 A 先生二十年，可以擔保他的品德和人格。

Courteous, patient and tactful, Mr. A is well-liked and respected by the staff. He is always punctual and dependable.

A 先生有禮貌，有耐心，注意言談技巧，受到員工們的喜愛和尊敬。他也十分守時和可靠。

Mr. B always practices what he preaches. With his pleasant disposition, he has excellent relations with other co-workers.

B 先生一向言行一致。由於有親切的個性，他與同仁相處十分良好。

He is a man who thinks of others and does not think only of himself. He is a bright student, but even beyond that, a fine, splendid, socially-minded human being.

他是一位老為別人，不只為自己著想的人。他是位聰明的學生，尤其更是一位令人高度讚賞合群的人。

During the past ten years. I have found him to be a man of fine character, with a sense of honesty and integrity. He is always willing to accept responsibility.

過去十年來，我發現他的品格很好，誠實而廉正。他總是願意承擔責任。

He has strong verbal and written communication skills and an ability to work with almost anyone.

他有很棒的說和寫的表達技巧，也有與任何人共事的能力。

Miss Lee's graciousness and unfailing kingness endear her to her associates, while her fine character, sincerity and high ideals have won their respect.

李小姐的親切和永恆的慈愛，使她受到同仁的喜歡；她的優良品格，真誠與崇高理念也贏得他們的尊敬。

He is such a friendly and modest person that social or intellectual snobbishness has no place with him. Students meet him gladly and faculty members enjoy his companionship.

他是一位友愛而謙虛的人，沒有社會上或學術上的自負心理。學生們高興見到他，教師們喜歡與他共事。

Mr. A is aware of his strengths and frankly admits his weak points. He willingly surrenders to those with greater knowledge and experience. He strives actively for self-improvement.

A 先生知道他的長處，也能誠實地承認自己的短處。他對那些有更多知識和經驗的人，願意讓步；他主動地努力改善自己。

（也有人用 development opportunity 代替 weak point）

With his magnetic personality, humorous expressions and wisdom, he is an outstanding figure among his associates.

他有磁性般的個性，幽默的談吐和智慧，他在同仁中，是位傑出的人物。

What I particularly admire about Mr. A is how he can retain his humor under a considerable amount of stress.

我對 A 先生特別羨慕的是他能在極大的壓力下，仍能保持幽默。

He is a tireless worker and an inspiring person. His co-workers have often turned to him for advice and cooperation. I have no doubt that he is an individual of incredible character.

他是一位孜孜不倦，激勵人心的人；他的同仁常常請他提供意見和合作。我想毫無疑問他是位極有品格的人。

Mr. A is a good caring young man who shows great concern and warmth for those around him. He is willing to give of himself to help others without expecting anything in return.

A 先生是位對他周邊的人十分關心和熱情的青年。他願以忘我的精神幫助他人，不求回報。

Among Mr. B's many attributes are his pleasant personality, courteous manners, quick-witted intelligence and genuine honesty.

A 先生的許多特點包括他令人喜歡的個性，禮貌的態度，敏銳的智慧，和至誠的正直。

With his friendly manner and congenial personality, it was always a pleasure to have him in my class.

他有友愛態度和令人愉快的性格，能有他在我班上是件樂事。

Miss A is widely known throughout our company for her warmth, her concern and kindness in dealing with her co-workers. She is not only a personable person, but also a capable and knowledgeable one.

A 小姐對同仁的熱情、關懷和友善，我們公司眾所皆知。她不但討人喜歡，也是一位能幹有見識的人。

Although I am not familiar with his employment record, I can assure you that he is a creative, intelligent, well-organized and cooperative young man.

雖然我不清楚他的就業紀錄，但我向你保證，他是位有創造性，聰明，有組織能力，並且合作的青年。

You will also find his personality most pleasing and he gets along unusually well with his fellow staff members.

你也能發覺他的性格十分討人喜歡；他與同事相處更是和諧。

I always enjoy my association with Mr. A. He was resourceful and thorough in everything and willing to accept criticism, to learn and to correct any fault.

我很喜歡與 A 先生共事，他對什麼事都很機敏和周全。他願意接受批評、學習，和改進任何錯誤。

In my estimation, he is a fine young man with a solid family background, who is a warm and caring person with a kind heart.

在我的估量中，他是位具有穩固家庭背景的好青年，也是熱誠、體貼、心地善良的人。

She is a young lady of charming personality and I am sure you will enjoy her company. Her warm smile, her light heart, and her infectious wit have always impressed me.

她是位具有可愛性格的青少女，我相信你會喜歡與她共事。她那熱情的笑容，興高采烈的心情，和那有感染力的風趣，總讓我印象深刻。

（light heart＝cheerful heart）

Her quiet manner, consistent poise and compassion for others are evident to those who work with her. She is so unique that she always gives of herself without counting the cost.

她舉止沉默，一貫鎮定並且對人熱情，顯然是她同仁的觀感。她經常不顧一切，獻身自己，確是難能可貴。

No one has worked in this department with such devotion and dedication as Mr. A. He has performed his duties with the attention and exactitude.

在本處工作的，沒有人像 A 先生這樣熱心和奉獻；他專心一意，嚴謹精確地執行他的職責。

His love of learning, high standard of conduct and sincere belief in unselfish service affect everyone privileged to work with him.

他愛好學習、高水平的行為，以及深信無私的服務影響到周邊有幸與他共事的每一位。

Mr. A's kindness, generosity and sense of humor have made him very dear to all of us. We appreciate his outstanding personality and unusual service to this department.

A 先生的親切、慷慨和幽默感，受到我們大家的喜愛。我們感謝他對本處的傑出個性與非凡的服務。

It is my impression that Mr. A is trustworthy and dependable. He is a man of stability and good character. Although I cannot evaluate his technical and professional competence, I feel sure that he would prove to be an extremely hard-working and dedicated employee.

我認為 A 先生可信又可靠。他是位很穩定，性格好的人。雖然我不想評估他技術性和專業性的能力，但我覺得他是非常努力熱誠的員工。

His tact, magnetic personality and profound knowledge of modern teaching methods have made him an ideal instructor.

他的言行技巧，吸引人的個性，以及對現代教學方法的豐富知識，使他成為一位理想的教師。

He is a truly gifted engineer and I have great respect for his high-quality work and his responsible and trustworthy character.

他真正是位有天分的工程師，我對他高水平的工作和他負責守信的性格，非常尊敬。

Although my association with Mr. A has been limited to several months, I have a favorable impression on him. I consider him a person with high tone of character, integrity and willingness to help others.

雖然我與 A 先生相處只有幾個月，但我對他印象很好，我認為他的品格高尚，剛正不阿，樂意助人。

Because she exhibits a very warm and pleasant personality, Miss A is loved and respected immensely by our faculty and student body.

由於 A 小姐有親切和藹的個性，她受到全體師生高度的愛戴和尊敬。

For nearly ten years, Mr. A has devoted his effort and energy to the interest of our school. His work is wide-reaching and his service is unselfish and far-sighted.

將近十年來，A 先生為我們學校的福利付出心力，他的工作，具有深遠影響，他的服務是大公無私，且有先見之明。

His devoted interest, wise counsel and loyal support are invaluable to us. His leaving is our loss but your gain.

他那專注的興趣，明智的協商，以及忠心的支持，對我們是很寶貴的。他的離職是我們的損失，而是你們的收穫。

I could never have completed my project without his assistance and he was always ready to hear my problems. I could count on him and feel sure that he would give his best efforts to your organization.

我如果沒有他的幫忙，不可能完成我的計畫；他隨時傾聽我的難題，我很信賴他，相信他對貴單位，也會做出最大的努力。

In concrete terms, Mr. A expresses the ideals of civilized conduct that can be translated into the human relationships of everyday life. He is a splendid, brilliant and outstanding gentleman.

明確地說，A 先生展現有教養的行為，已說明了日常生活的人際關係。他是位值得讚揚，聰明而彬彬有禮的人。

Mr. A worked tirelessly and efficiently during the years he was with us and I found him completely trustworthy in every respect.

A 先生與我們共事幾年來，我發現他孜孜不倦，一直工作效率很高。他在各方面都是完全可以信任的。

He is a man of seemingly boundless energy. He maintains a strong output of work and responds to pressure without loss of poise.

他似乎是位精力無窮的男士；他能保持工作的高產量，且能從容面對壓力。

He is exceedingly generous with his time and energy. He is always accessible and ready to help any of us solve a problem.

他非常大方地獻出時間與精力；他很容易與人接近，隨時幫助我們解決問題。

Mr. A will be greatly missed not only for his knowledge and hardwork, but also for his cheerful attitude and ability to get along well with others.

A 先生會受到人們的懷念，不但因為他的知識與勤奮，也因為他那種令人愉悅的態度，和與人合諧相處的能力。

With her cheerful personality and a sense of humor, Miss A always puts others before herself, and wears a smile on her face.

A 小姐具有令人喜悅的性格和幽默感，她經常把別人列為優先，並面帶笑容。

Whenever we need Mr. A, he always offers his unselfish assistance. The faithful way he is aiding our department has reassured all of us. We have benefited much from his selflessness and generosity.

只要我們需要 A 先生，他總是無私的幫忙。他忠心耿耿地協助本單位，使我們全體同仁放心；他的慷慨和無私，使我們受益良多。

During the past ten years, his cooperation and dedication to fine teaching has been deeply appreciated. It is partly due to his efforts that our school has had fruitful years.

過去十年來，他對出色教學的合作與奉獻，受到高度讚賞。我們學校近年來成果豐碩，部分歸功於他的努力。

Mr. A always tries to serve and to give of himself and asks nothing in return. Also, he has shared his expertise, wit and warmth with our department.

A 先生奮不顧身地設法幫助他人，且不求回報。他也與本單位分享他的專長、風趣和熱情。

He is always willing to give up his free time for others. He does not focus on himself, but enriches other people's lives.

他常願意為他人放棄他的空閒時間；他不把焦點放在自己身上，而是想要充實他人生活。

Miss A is a creative and enthusiastic teacher with a strong service-oriented desire. She has leadership ability, organizational skills and problem-solving capacity.

A 小姐是位有創造性、熱心、且有強烈服務慾望的老師。她有領導能力、組織技能和解決問題的幹練。

He gives as much of his time as people request whenever they need assistance. He creates a trusting and open atmosphere where individual suggestions are welcomed among staff.

只要有人需要他的幫忙，他總是給人家所要的時間。他創造一個可信而開放的氣氛，接納同事的個人建議。

Mr. A's service-oriented attitude, his friendliness and his concern for the people he worked with, were as valuable to this department as his computer expertise.

A 先生那種熱心服務的態度、他的友愛和對他的同事的關懷，如同他的電腦專長一樣，對本單位至為珍貴。

I can honestly say that I have never worked with anyone who is more industrious, cooperative or more dedicated to his profession.

老實說，我從來沒有與任何人共事像他這樣對專業如此的勤奮、合作和奉獻。

Working five years with Mr. A has revealed a man who is deeply interested in providing the best of himself to his job. He takes a step beyond service care for others.

與 A 先生共事五年，發現他很有興趣對他工作做最大的付出；他對別人的服務關懷，總是搶先人一步。

The loyalty and devotion Mr. A displayed over an extended period merit my commendation. I am truly impressed by his unhesitating effort on behalf of our school.

A 先生在那段很長時間所表現的忠誠和奉獻，值得我的讚美。我對他為我們學校所做的堅定努力，至誠感動。

Mr. B extends his association with students beyond the classroom and expands his activities to include community services, in which he has demonstrated his skills in working with the diverse interests of people.

B 先生與學生的交流超出課堂範圍；他的活動包括社區服務，展現出他與不同興趣人群工作的技巧。

She has a way of working with people that stimulates support and industry. Her unfailing poise, generosity and kindness enable her to make many friends.

她有一種能激勵他人支持和努力的方法；她那一貫的鎮靜，慷慨和愛心，使她交到許多朋友。

His participation in various school activities has made him well-known on the campus, while his sportsmanlike attitude and contagious enthusiasm endear him to all who play or work with him.

他參加不同的學校活動，使他在校園中成名；他具有運動家的風度，和感染性的熱心，使與他共處的人，都喜歡他。

學歷與經歷（Education and experience）

　　學歷與經歷在履歷表（resume）裡，通常已說得很清楚，在推薦信中，可以不必重提。如果要，也可輕描淡寫地說：

His schooling and previous job background should have prepared him well for this position.

他的學校教育和過去工作背景，應該十分適合這份工作。

From Mr. A's excellent records in school, I am certain he will be successful in whatever career he pursues.

以 A 先生在校的優良成績，我深信他不管做什麼，都能成功。

Having taken several management training courses, he has gained skills and capabilities in working with and supervising employees.

他選修幾門管理訓練課程，取得與人共事和督導員工的技巧和才能。

With five years of professional experience and two advanced academic degrees, Mr. A will bring the functional and technical skills required for this job description.

A 先生以五年的專業經驗和兩個高學位，將會帶來這份工作所需的功能性和專門性技術。

Her outstanding educational background and six-year computer experience have been reflected in her accomplishment at our department.

她傑出的教育背景和六年的電腦經驗，可從她在本部門的成績反映出來。

Miss A's MBA from Harvard University and her five years of counseling experience qualify her to teach leadership courses in your college.

A 小姐從哈大取得企管碩士學位和五年的諮詢經驗，使她夠資格為你們大學講授領導才能課程。

Mr. A has spent his entire twenty-year career in the public school system. He will bring to the job an interesting combination of personal and professional qualifications and experiences.

A 先生的職涯有二十年在公立學校；他將為工作注入個人和專業上的資歷和經驗。

His excellent academic achievements will insure him to be a competent researcher in your organization.

他在學術上的優秀成績，能保證他在貴單位會是一位勝任的研究員。

With a Master's degree in math and a Ph. D in computer science, I know professor A can make some contributions to your college.

A 教授擁有數學碩士、電腦博士學位，我相信他對貴校能有一些貢獻。

Mr. B will bring a real bonus in the form of a Master's degree in business administration.

B 先生的企管碩士學位，將帶來實際額外的好處。

His credentials including a degree in business management appear to have what is needed to hit the ground running.

他的文憑包括一個企業管理的學位，似乎具備大展鴻圖所需的條件。

(to hit the ground running 的意思是 to begin at full speed)

工作表現（**Work performance**）

包括工作能力，專業技術以及成就、得獎等。這也是老外十分重視的。我大致分為兩方面來說：

1. 文教人員

Mr. A strikes me as a competent teacher. He demonstrates scholarship in his specialized field. He aspires to further his knowledge by extending his education.

A 先生是位稱職的教師，給我深刻的印象。在他專門領域裡，展現出學術方面的成就。藉著延伸他的教育，他追求更深的知識。

She is a dedicated classroom teacher and is recognized for her enthusiasm and creativity. She was an active participant in, spokesperson for, and advocate of the high-tech program.

她是一位認真的教師；她的熱心和創造力，受到表彰。她為高科技的計畫熱心投入，是其代言人和倡導者。

His variety of experience as a teacher / librarian gives him a comprehensive understanding of the educational field.

他從事教師／圖書館專業員的不同經驗，帶給他在教育領域裡廣泛的認識。

Mr. A's imaginative presentation in the classroom has established a rapport between students and himself. He is very active in planning various programs on campus.

A 先生在班上富於想像力的講授，使他與學生間建立了融洽的關係。他在校園內非常積極計畫各種不同的活動。

I had several occasions to discuss with him some problems in teaching special education. It impressed me that he has a thorough knowledge of teaching techniques.

在幾個場合中，我與他討論特殊教育的問題；他對教學技巧的全面知識，令我印象深刻。

He provided superior leadership in the area of curriculum development for our school. He demonstrated exceptional ability to motivate and inspire other faculty to work as a team.

他為我們學校的課程進展，提供高水平的領導；他激勵其他教師的團隊精神，表現了傑出的才能。

As a researcher at this college. Mr. A proved to be well above average in competence and professionalism. He always provided more than what might be expected of him.

身為本大學的研究員，A 先生的工作勝任和專業作風，是超乎平常的。他所提供的，往往多過所期待的。

Students evaluated Mr. A as an outstanding teacher and role model who fostered critical thinking and inspired students to excel in the discipline.

學生們評價 A 先生是位傑出的教師，也是供人仿效的榜樣；他培養學生認真思考，並鼓勵學生學業精進。

As a leader in the student government and a very efficient class president, his ideas and energies for projects seem inexhaustible.

身為一位學生會領導人和高效率的班主席，他對各項方案的想法和幹勁，似乎用之不竭。

Working as student counselor for five years, I can say that no previous SGA president has come close to his leadership ability.

我擔任了五年的學生輔導，可以說過去沒有學生會主席能與他的領導能力接近。

Since Miss A enrolled in our accelerated academic program, she has excelled. There is no challenge too difficult for her to accomplish in a short period of time.

自從 A 小姐參加我們速成學術計畫以來，她表現突出。對她而言，沒有什麼太難的挑戰是她不能在短期內完成的。

It is obvious to anyone who looks at her transcript that Miss A is an outstanding student. Ranking first in her class is surely no small accomplishment.

任何人看到 A 小姐的成績單，就能明顯地看出她是位傑出的學生。她列為班上第一名，不是小小的成就。

Mr. A has achieved straight A's for three years while taking courses with one of the most challenging curricula offered.

A 先生選修一些最富挑戰性的課程，而取得三年全 A 的成績。

As a graduate student. Mr. B has secured two grants for his researches. He was recently named to the scholars list for obtaining a 4.0 GPA during the fall semester.

身為一位研究生，B 先生獲得兩項研究助學金。由於他秋季的平均成績達到 4.0，他最近被列在學者名單上。

In my class. I found Miss B to be a model student. Her work was of a consistently high quality. She regularly participated in class discussion and was never afraid to ask questions.

在我班上，我發現 B 小姐是位模範生：她的學業經常是高品質。她定時參加班上討論，不怕提出問題。

When I think about Mr. A, immediately the words "outstanding" and "extraordinary", come to my mind. He entered our university as a freshman and has demonstrated as a mature and responsible young man, superior scholastic achievement and leadership qualities.

當我想起 A 先生，「優秀」、 「卓越」的字眼，馬上浮現我腦海中。他進入本大學只是大一新生，但他表現成熟、負責的青年，並且具有優異的學術成就和領導的品質。

Currently serving as math teacher, Miss A has brought her expertise in this field and has made a distinct contribution to our school.

目前 A 小姐身為數學教師，她在這方面帶來她的專門知識，也對本校做出一項顯著的貢獻。

He has distinguished himself in several school and community organizations both scholastically oriented as well as extracurricular. Another milestone in his accomplishment was that he represented our school for the International Student Conference in London.

他參加數次學校和社區的學術和課外活動，表現得很出色。他的成就另一個里程碑就是代表我們學校參加在倫敦的國際學生會議。

He received accolades from students for his classroom teaching and for the interest and support he showed them. He continues to do a good job, accepting new teaching assignments graciously.

他課堂上的教學和對學生的興趣與支持，得到學生們的讚美。他依然工作表現良好，欣然接受新的教學任務。

Mr. A has brought a rich breadth and depth of expertise to his classes. He fosters growth and responsibility in his students' learning.

A 先生帶給他班上廣泛且有深度的專門知識：他促進學生學習上的成長與責任感。

Her teaching evaluations are among the most laudatory in this department. She currently has three research articles in press.

她的教學評量，在本系是最受頌揚者之一。他目前有三篇研究的文章，即將發表。

Because of his expertise in lab organization and safety, Mr. B was invited to instruct in several workshops. He has assisted science teachers and served as a high school science advisor.

由於 B 先生對實驗室的體制和安全具有專長，他在數次研討會中，被邀請講授。他協助科技教師，也擔任高中科技的顧問。

Through his research, Mr. A has acquired a good reputation in the field of food science. He also has an extensive list of lecturing activities in which he participates on and off campus.

A 先生在食品科學的研究領域裡，極富盛名美譽。他也參加一連串的校內外講演活動。

His students view him as an excellent teacher who always does his best to help them. Many of those students comment on the great amount to be learned in his classes.

他的學生認為他是一位傑出的老師：他經常盡力幫助他們，許多學生稱許在他班上，可學到不少東西。

Over the years Miss A has developed a deeply personal philosophy as a teacher. Her goal is always to help her students in English literature.

多年來，A 小姐的人生觀就是要做一位老師。她的目標，就是在英語文學方面，幫助她的學生。

Mr. A is energetic, animated and well-versed in the subject matter he teaches. He is committed and dedicated to the mission of high quality teaching.

A 先生有幹勁，生氣勃勃，和精通他所教的科目；他忠心耿耿，獻身於高品質的教學。

As a scholar librarian, he worked with students on several research projects. He was the recipient of many honors from professional societies, and wrote many articles on information science.

身為學者圖書館專業員，他與學生合作幾項研究計畫。他從專業協會獲得多種表揚，同時也寫了許多資訊科學的文章。

Mr. B is an outstanding addition to our history faculty and his research productivity continues to be exemplary.

B 先生是我們歷史教師中傑出的新力量：他的研究富有成效，堪作楷模。

He is one of the most dynamic and innovative math teacher one can imagine. Both formal and informal feedback on his teaching make him among the top in our department.

他是位想像中最有活力，最有創新的教師之一。由正式和非正式的反應結果，他的教學，是系裡列入最棒之中。

Mr. A is often described by students and faculty as a gifted educator. His success stems from his ability to motivate students in learning.

A 先生常被學生和教師們認為是位天才教育家：他的成功是基於鼓勵學生學習的才能。

She challenges her students to achieve high levels of performance. This is followed by her continuous support and encouragement until the student's work comes to fruition.

她挑戰學生達到高水平的成績；隨之又繼續支持和鼓勵，直到學生取得成果為止。

As head of the department, I have worked closely with Mr. A and have observed his ability to perform his job for the benefit of our school. He has ably led his research team in the fulfillment of our mission.

身為本處主任，我與 A 先生工作密切，並且看到他的工作能力，都為本校的利益著想。他精明地帶領他的研究小組，完成我們的任務。

His strategies of innovation, classroom presentation and feedback are very effective. His knowledge of social science is seemingly encyclopedic.

他革新的策略，課堂的講解和反應，都很有成效。他對社會科學的知識似乎十分廣博。

He is the kind of faculty member who does it all and does it well. Particularly remarkable about him is the extent of his community service.

他是那種什麼都做，而且做得很好的教師。尤其引人注目的是他對社區服務的程度。

Mr. A displays strengths in teaching as indicated by his annual evaluations. His creative teaching strategies grow out of his constant commitment.

A 先生的年度評估，顯示他在教學方面的特別實力；他的創造性教學策略，係來自他持續的投入。

His enthusiasm and caring in teaching is rated excellent by every instrument we have available. He successfully submitted a paper for presentation at a prestigious conference.

他的教學熱忱和關懷，我們用各種方式評估，都是一流。他在一次有知名度的研討會中，完滿地提出一篇書面報告。

Miss A has a talent in persuasive speaking and she impressed me and many other faculty members. In working with her, I have nothing but praise for her.

A 小姐有說服人的口才，她讓我和其他許多教師留下深刻的印象。與她一起工作，我沒有別的，只有讚揚她。

Having been his colleague for ten years, I can say that he could give lessons on how to be an ideal teacher.

與他同事十年，我敢說他能開課教授如何做個理想的老師。

He continues his role as an exemplary faculty member in computer science. Three of his papers were accepted for presentation at important computer meetings.

他在電腦科技方面，繼續扮演模範教師的角色。他的三篇文章，在重要電腦會議中，通過發表。

In my ten-year career, I have never known a student who has so completely exhibited the qualities of scholarship, leadership and integrity.

在我十年的經歷中，我從未見過一位學生是這麼完全地表現出高品質的學術成就、領導才能和剛正不阿。

As the first Chinese teacher at this school, Mr. Chen has always been respected by students. His insights have helped many students find their ways to a quality education.

陳先生是本校首位的中國教師，他常常受到學生尊敬。他的洞察能力，幫助許多學生找到優質教育的途徑。

Serving as a student advisor, Mr. A helped many students feel a part of the institution. His students fondly consider him as a taskmaster.

A 先生身為學生顧問，幫助許多學生感到屬於學校的一部分。他的學生認為他是一位嚴格的督導者。

As a library student assistant, Mr. A's main duties included bibliographic searching and indexing to provide subject entries. He has been a very diligent worker and has willingly accepted detailed assignments.

A 先生是圖書館的學生助手，他的主要工作，包括目錄的搜查和索引，以提供主詞的條目。他工作很努力，並且願意接受細節的任務。

As an instructor, Mr. A has proved to be extremely capable and responsible. He has demonstrated initiative, resourcefulness and competence. His students' response to their learning experience with him has always been positive.

A 先生做為一位講師，證明非常能幹和負責；他表現出進取、機敏和勝任，他的學生與他學習經驗的反應，一直很正面。

Over the past ten years. Mr. A was responsible for all engineering designs. I would like to commend him on the contribution he has made to the success of our design project.

過去十年來，A 先生負責所有的工程設計；我很讚賞他對我們設計方案的貢獻。

Professor A published many articles in both national and international journals. He also serves our college tirelessly as a member of several committees.

A 教師在國內和國際刊物裡，發表過許多文章，他也在我們大學裡擔任幾個委員會的成員，不倦地服務。

Miss A is willing to work as hard herself as she expects others to work. She is the kind of student leader who makes my job easy.

A 小姐願意自己工作努力，就像她期待別人工作一樣。她是那種使我的工作不費力的學生領袖。

As Mr. A has positively influenced the lives of our students, our school recognized his accomplishments last year by a service award.

由於 A 先生對我們學生的生活有正面的影響，我們學校去年以服務獎表揚他的功績。

I have always found Mr. A a lucid, logical thinker and a faculty member willing to set and adhere to high personal and academic standards.

我常常發覺 A 先生是位明晰、邏輯清楚的思維者，也是一位願意制定個人和學術上高水平的教師。

He is active in many academic organizations and a very diligent instructor who has done an excellent job in teaching his math courses.

他在許多學術機構很活躍，也是十分勤奮的講師。他講授數學課程也很出色。

Mr. A remains a dynamic teacher and brings the most recent advances in science to his classroom instruction. He continues to be an active member of several school-wide committees.

A 先生一直是一位有活力的老師，他帶給他班上教學最新的科技。他還是幾個校際委員會的活躍成員之一。

He is a very able and hard-working researcher, well qualified to manage a research team.

他是位十分能幹而努力的研究員，他夠資格帶領一個研究小組。

Mr. A is a dedicated teacher who provided his students the unique and valuable experience of going on research trips several times.

A 先生是位熱誠的老師，他數次的研究旅行，提供他學生獨特寶貴的經驗。

In my opinion, Mr. B has done a fine job in committing himself to research and writing. His teaching evaluations are outstanding and he is an asset to our computer program.

以我個人意見，B 先生投入研究與寫作表現良好。他的教學評估非常優秀。他是我們電腦計畫中的人才。

2. 一般人員：

例如：

Since my daily routine is closely associated with Mr. A's department, I have had many opportunities to judge the quality of his work.

由於我每天的工作與 A 先生的部門有密切聯繫，所以我有許多機會評估他的工作品質。

He is competent, cooperative, responsible, alert and an intelligent person. His ability to make suggestions in problem-solving has become a boon to our department.

他是能幹、合作、負責、敏捷且聰明的人。他能建議解決問題的本領，是我們部門得力之才。

He possesses a very bright mind and is a diligent and careful worker. He is always willing to do more than the assigned task (requires).

他具有十分聰明的腦筋，而且是位努力而仔細的員工。他常常願意做超越他指派的工作。

Miss A is always just and kind in the treatment of others, calm in excitement, wise in decision and quick in action.

A 小姐對待他人很公正親切；激動時能冷靜，決定事情很明智，採取行動也很迅速。

His broad business background includes tax preparation, cash flow, sales analysis and marketing research. He works equally effectively with his superiors, his peers and his subordinates.

他的廣博商業底子包括稅務準備，現金流轉，銷售分析和市場研究。他與上司、同仁和部屬共事，也很調和。

Mr. A is extremely skillful, a quick and accurate thinker. I believe he will prove to be a capable and dependable employee.

A 先生非常精巧，也是一位敏銳正確的思考者。我相信他將是位能幹可靠的員工。

It did not take us long to know that Mr. A's abilities were far in excess of the demands of the job assigned to him.

我們不需要長時間就知道，A先生的能力大大超過他所指定的工作。

In the years I have known Mr. A, I have become aware of his hard work, his professional attitude and his leadership potential.

多年來我認識 A 先生，知道他工作努力，有專業態度，以及有領導的潛力。

Although his duties were mainly semi-professional, I respect his accuracy, thoroughness and capacity for hard work. He works tirelessly and most efficiently. His tact is unquestionable and his ability topnotch.

雖然他的職責主要是半專業性，但我對他在困難工作上的精確、徹底和幹練，倒很敬重。他不倦的工作，很有效率；他的機敏是受肯定的，他的才能是一流的。

His progressive planning, tireless industry and keen judgment have helped to make our department one of the best in the field.

他先進的籌畫，不斷的努力和敏銳的判斷，使我們部門成為這個領域裡最棒的一員。

Being diligent, efficient, responsible and alert, Mr. A performed his job very well.

A 先生是勤奮、能幹、負責和機智的人；他的工作表現良好。

His energy and intelligence have been a great asset to this department. I have found him to be irreplaceable, invaluable and indispensable.

他的精力和才智是本單位的寶貝。我發現他是不能替代的，非常可貴的，也是不可缺少的。

As an employee of this company, Mr. A has given much not only through the diligent performance of his duties, but also in his commitment to our community service.

A 先生身為本公司的員工，他不但從勤奮的職責中獻身付出，且對社區服務，也相當投入。

Mr. A served in our department with distinction and is highly respected in his field by his colleagues.

A 先生在本單位服務非常傑出：在他領域裡，受到同事高度的尊重。

I appreciate his many contributions to the betterment of this division. Every worthwhile cause and project has received his vigorous and wholehearted support for which I am very grateful.

我謝謝他對本部門的改善做出許多貢獻。每個值得做的事情與方案，都得到他全心全力的支持，這點我很感激。

He is a super-organizer and seems to have boundless energy and enthusiasm. Because of his long and tireless efforts, our department has become a better place to work.

他是位超棒的組織者，似乎有無限的精力和熱情。由於他長期不斷的努力，我們單位成員有更好的工作場地。

During his career with this company, he has held increasingly responsible positions. His contributions have added a great deal to the success of our operations.

他在本公司服務期間，擔任多項重要的工作。他的貢獻，添增不少我們業務的成功。

As a former director of the department, I can honestly say that I have never worked with anyone who is more industrious, more ambitious or more capable in his job.

身為本部門前任的主任，我誠懇地說，我從未與一位這麼勤勞，這麼有雄心，這麼能幹的人一同工作。

（為了加強語氣，故用三個 more）

I regard Mr. A highly as a person of integrity and dedication to his responsibilities. He definitely is a man of professional competence, personal strength and versatility.

A 先生是位廉正獻身職責的人，我很敬愛他。他絕對也是一位專業稱職，有個人活力和多才多藝的人。

During those years with us, I have found him completely trustworthy in every respect. His vision, judgment and courageous conviction have influenced our decisions and buoyed up our spirits.

他與我們共事多年以來，我發覺他在各方面都可信賴。他的眼光，判斷和勇於認錯，左右了我們的決定、鼓舞了我們的精神。

He is superior in the ability to think rapidly and accurately, He has skill in detecting major factors in complex situation.

他迅速而正確的思考能力，十分優秀。他對複雜情況，能技巧地查出重要因素。

Over the past five years, Mr. A has proved to be a remarkable young man who combined all the qualities necessary to make him a topnotch employee.

過去五年來，A 先生證明是位出色的青年。他具有一流員工應備的所有特質。

Mr. A has performed his work in both a conscientious and accurate manner. He has demonstrated a sincere interest in his work and maintains a professional attitude toward it.

A 先生對工作既認真又準確；他表現對他工作的興趣，同時保持對工作的專業態度。

When Mr. A initiates a project or an idea, he will work tirelessly to see it through to a successful result.

當 A 先生開始一個方案或想法時，他會孜孜不倦地工作，直到看到成功的結果。

Seeing Mr. B at work was instructive and inspiring. He could make the most demanding tasks bearable.

看到 B 先生在工作，是有啟發性和激勵人心的。他能承受最嚴苛的任務。

Not only is he skillful in face-to-face contacts, but he also expresses his ideas clearly and forcefully.

他不但與人當面接觸有技巧，而且表達意見很明白和有力。

With his extensive background in business administration, I am certain Mr. A will find many opportunities to use his talents and capabilities.

以他廣泛的企管背景，我相信 A 先生有很多機會使用他的天分和才華。

It is difficult for me to describe this outstanding and dynamic young lady. However, I do envision her as having career success. I predict a great future for her.

我很難描寫這位傑出有活力的年輕淑女。但我可展望她在事業上的成就。我預料她有個美好的未來。

In addition to many commendations and notes of thanks for her services over the years, Miss A received three outstanding performance ratings.

除了對 A 小姐許多書面的表彰和謝函外，她還得到三次傑出業績的評分。

In recognition of his sustained contributions to this organization, we presented Mr. A a Superior Service Award in 2008.

2008 年我們頒發 A 先生傑出服務獎，以表彰他為本機構持續的貢獻。

It is my deep personal satisfaction to have worked with Mr. A during the past ten years, and I will always cherish his support and friendship.

過去十年來，能與 A 先生共事，是我個人最大的滿足。我會珍惜他的支持和友誼。

His background, experience and tactfulness have made him ideally suited for this position. I believe he'll bring credit to himself and will carry out his duties with industry and fidelity.

他的背景、經驗和機敏，使他十分適合這份職務。我相信他會為自己增光，也會以勤奮和忠誠執行他的任務。

Mr. A is a gentleman and a leader beloved by all his associates. At the same time, he will give of himself to make your company a better place.

A 先生是位受到他全體同仁敬愛的紳士和領袖；同時，他會獻身自己，使貴公司成為更好的場所。

His contributions to this organization have been far-reaching and profound. We would await his return to our department if one day he so desires.

他對本機構的貢獻,影響深遠而廣泛。如果有一天他想再回本單位,我們會期待他的來臨。

I have been amazed with his ability to learn not just our company system, but our community as well in such a short period of time.

他有能力在短短時間內,不僅學到我們公司的制度,也能了解我們的社區,令我驚異。

She is alert to her duties and tireless in her pursuit of them. As a staff member in this department, she has been eminently satisfactory.

她對她的職責很警惕,並且不斷地追求達成任務。她身為本處職員,我們對她的表現極為滿意。

He is superior in organizing his work and in directing the work of others. He has the capacity to plan complex operations.

他對自己的工作和督導他人的工作,都非常有條理;他對處理複雜的業務也具能力。

He enlists effective cooperation from his staff, and gives credit to those whom he directs. He makes a team of his workers and people like to play on his team.

他贏得他員工有效的合作,並對那些他指導的人給予讚揚。他把員工組成團隊,大家樂意彼此配合。

She has received several official recognitions for her resourcefulness and conscientious work at this company.

由於她的機敏和認真工作，她得到本公司數次正式的表揚。

Endowed with good judgment and ability, Mr. A received a number of special citations. Throughout his career as a diligent and conscientious employee, he has risen through the ranks.

A 先生天生具有良好的判斷和本領，他收到多項特別的表揚。在他事業的過程中，他是位工作努力和認真的員工，他的職位步步高升。

Although his stay with us was brief, we were pleased with his performance. He acted responsibly and conscientiously at all time, and we were sorry to have him leave so soon.

雖然他與我們共事的時間很短，但我們滿意他的工作表現；他一向負責認真，他這麼快離職，我們感到遺憾。

Over the years, Mr. A acquired a wealth of knowledge in computer software and familiarity with current needs in the field.

多年來，A 先生在電腦軟體方面獲得豐富知識；他對這領域的最新需求也很熟悉。

I have had the privilege of knowing and working with Mr. A for many years. He has demonstrated great skills as an engineer, never backing down from difficult problems.

多年來我有幸認識 A 先生與他共事：他身為一位工程師，展現了高度的技能，遇到困難問題從不退卻。

Mr. A is practical and flexible on issues relating to procedures, processes and methods. He is a willing and capable employee who has a thorough knowledge of computer programming.

A 先生對議題的程序、步驟和方法，十分實際而有彈性。他是一位樂意肯幹的員工，對電腦程式的知識極為貫通。

Mr. B was with us only a few months and left us before we had an opportunity to judge him well. He seemed, however, a very pleasant young man who made an excellent appearance.

B 先生與我們相處只有幾個月就離開了；我們沒有機會對他深入了解；不過在外表上，他似乎是位令人喜愛的年輕人。

Her skills and capabilities in working with and supervising other employees are excellent. She will be missed for her dedication, cooperation and willingness to help others.

她的工作技能和才華以及對其他員工的督導，均屬一流。她的獻身精神與合作，還有幫助他人的意願，將會受到懷念。

Mr. A is a first-class programmer, most careful about the minutest detail of his work. He is also good at system analysis and personnel management.

A 先生是一流的程式員，對他工作洞察秋毫。他對系統分析和人事管理也很高明。

There is nothing about him that is average. He excels in whatever he does. We benefited from his cooperation and support.

對他而言，沒有事只是普普通通；他不管做什麼都很傑出。我們從他的合作和支持，受益良多。

He has made a number of significant contributions to our department. His professional skills have improved substantially during the past years.

他為本部門做了多項有意義的貢獻。過去幾年來，他的專業技能進步相當多。

It is no exaggeration to say that his performance not only exceeds normal requirements but deserves special commendation.

他的工作表現，不但超過一般要求，也值得特別表揚，這種說法並非誇張。

結尾語（Summary or conclusion）

這是對被推薦者總結意見，或願意提供其他資料。

例如：

Mr. A will be a valued employee from every point of view. Whatever he seeks to do, he will do well.

從各方面來看，A 先生是位難能可貴的員工；不管他想做什麼，他都會做得很好。

I am confident that Mr. B would be an asset to any firm that can use his services.

我有信心，B 先生對任何能聘用他的公司，都是難得之才。

I recommend Mr. A most highly for any position for which he qualifies, believing that he will be great gain to his prospective employer.

我高度推薦 A 先生擔任他合適的任何工作；相信他會使未來的雇主大大受益。

Any kind assistance you may extend to Mr. B will be highly appreciated.

你對 B 先生的任何友愛幫助，將會受到高度的感激。

I hope you will give Mr. A, to the best of your ability, the assistance he is seeking.

我希望你能對 A 先生的請求，盡最大力量給予協助。

I am happy to recommend Mr. A and (will) be pleased to supply further information should it be required.

我很高興推薦 A 先生，如需更多資料，我也樂於提供。

I can unreservedly recommend Mr. B to anyone in need of a person with real math and computer talents.

我毫無保留地推薦 B 先生給任何需要真正有數學和電腦天賦的人。

I consider Mr. A eminently qualified for the position he is seeking in your office and entitled to your upmost confidence.

我認為 A 先生非常合適他在貴處所申請的工作，並且可以受到你最高度的信任。

（upmost＝uppermost）

At the same time I would recommend him without any reservation, to the highest degree, believing that he would be an asset to your organization.

同時，我毫無保留地高度推薦他，相信他將是貴單位得力之才。

I (heartily) commend him for the most favorable consideration of your institution.

我誠懇地推薦他給貴機構，希望能得到你們最好的考慮。

(commend＝recommend)

Happy, I can count Mr. A among the best members of my own staff, and at the same time, heartily recommend him (to you).

我很高興把 A 先生列入我自己最好的員工之中，同時熱誠地推薦給你。

I have no hesitation in recommending Mr. A for any responsibilities you may see fit to assign him.

我毫不猶豫地推薦 A 先生，負責任何你認為適合他的職務。

I believe your company would benefit immensely from his contributions.

我相信貴公司從他的貢獻中將會受益良多。

I take pleasure in recommending Miss A to you. Let me know if there is anything further I can offer.

我很高興向你推薦 A 小姐，如有其他我能提供的事，請告知。

I will be happy to answer any questions you may have about Mr. A.

我會很高興回答任何有關 A 先生的問題。

If I can provide additional information, please feel free to contact me.

假如我能提供其他資料，請隨時與我聯絡。

I am sure that Mr. A's proven capability in his field will be just what your company needs.

我相信 A 先生在他領域裡被證實的技能，也就是貴公司所需要的。

We would be sorry to lose such a dependable and accommodating employee as Mr. A. I wholeheartedly recommend him to you.

我們感到難過失去像 A 先生這樣可靠和樂於助人的員工。我全心全意把他推薦給你。

但也有不講這種結尾語或結論的形式，而是把信中的內容相配合，籠統地表示出來。例如：

It is my sincere belief that he will prove to be a fine worker. His personality, faith, friendliness and real liking for people should take him far.

我真誠相信他將是位好員工；他的品格、忠誠、友善和愛護他人，會帶給他成功。

（take him far＝make him a success）

Now that Mr. A has decided to resign his job, I will be the first to miss him at work, and the first to recommend him highly as a gentleman and as an excellent teacher.

既然 A 先生已決定辭職，我在工作中，將是首位想念他，也是首位高度推薦這位有教養的人，及傑出的教師。

I have no doubt that he will serve you well in his new endeavor. I wish him every success in his new post.

我毫不懷疑，他在新事業上能好好為你服務；我也祝福他新工作一切成功。

I feel what will mean most to Mr. A is the atmosphere of learning in your university. He will appreciate the opportunity to utilize his good brain to its capacity and to explore intellectual areas that are new to him.

我認為對 A 先生最有意義的是你們大學的學習環境。他會讚賞這個機會，使用他的智慧，去探討對他陌生的學術領域。

Miss A is serious about education and I am confident that she will be successful in your graduate school.

A 小姐對教育很認真，我有信心她就讀你們的研究所將會成功。

I can recommend Mr. A for any position requiring superior ability with computer and math knowledge.

我能推薦 A 先生給任何一個需要高度電腦和數學知識的工作。

Considering his excellent training, experience and pleasant personality, he would be a fine addition to your staff.

考慮到他最好的訓練和經驗，以及令人喜愛的性格，他將是你們員工中一位很好的新生力軍。

Therefore, I can recommend Mr. A enthusiastically as an intelligent man, a good worker and a man with a bright future.

所以我熱誠地推薦 A 先生，他是位有才智、工作勤奮，前途美好的人。

His background with our company has given Mr. A excellent training which makes him worth your favorable consideration.

A 先生在我們公司的經驗，得到最佳的訓練，值得你們有利的考慮。

Mr. B would be an asset to any organization in regard to high-tech challenges. I would appreciate any favorable consideration you can extend to him.

在高科技的挑戰方面，B 先生是任何機構的人才；我也感謝你對他有利的考慮。

Mr. A's schooling and previous job background should have prepared him for this position. His departure from this department left a vacuum in our creative planning.

A 先生的學校教育和過去工作經歷，會對這個職位，有所準備。他離開本部門，對於我們創意的計畫，留下了空白。

Mr. B would be a real addition to your organization not only because of his pleasing personality, but also because of his ability and intelligence.

B 先生將是貴機構一位真正的新生力軍，不但因為他有令人喜愛的個性，且因他有才能和智慧。

I believe Mr. A will continue to meet the challenges ahead with the same degree of dedication as he had in the past.

我相信 A 先生將會以他過去同樣的投入精神，繼續面對未來的挑戰。

It would be an excellent opportunity for Mr. B to increase his knowledge in this growing field and prepare himself for advancement should you grant him a chance to study in the U.S.

假如你能給 B 先生一個在美學習的機會，他將會在這日漸發展的領域裡增進知識，也為他自己的晉升有所準備。

There is so much more I could say about Miss A. Perhaps the best way to conclude is by saying that our school is a better place as a result of her being here.

關於 A 小姐，我有很多恭維要說，也許最好的結論就是，有她在這裡服務，使本校成為更好的工作場所。

After completing his advanced studies in the U.S., I believe Mr. A will become more valuable to China upon his return thereto.

A 先生在美深造後，我相信他回到中國將會更受重視。

(his return thereto＝return to his homeland)

I am confident that Mr. B will have a long and successful career in your organization.

我相信 B 先生在貴機構將有長期而成功的事業。

　　如要說明離職原因，也可輕描淡寫加上一句。

　　例如：

We terminated his employment because under our company's new policy, we laid off several full-time professionals in favor of part-time semi-professionals.

由於我們公司的新制度而結束他的工作。我們解聘數位全職專業人員，而聘用兼職專業人員。

As Mr. A refused to accept a part-time position, we had no other full-time opening for which he was qualified (at that time).

A先生不願接受兼職工作，而(那時)我們又沒有合適他的工作機會。

We would be sorry to see him go, but we understand his desire for a position that could offer more rapid advancement.

我們看到他離職很難過，不過我們理解他想找個能給他較快晉升的工作機會。

Mr. A left this department of his own volition for personal reasons.

A先生離開本部門，是因為他個人原因而做出的決定。

He was a valued employee from every point of view. The repercussions of his leaving will be felt across our campus.

從各方面來看，他是位難能可貴的員工，他的離職影響深遠，我們全校將有感受。

I believe Mr. A left us for family reasons. We would have him back with us again if there were an opening now.

我們相信 A 先生離開是因為家庭的原因。假如我們現在有空缺，還是希望他再回來。

I believe Mr. A left us to pursue a more challenging job opportunity.

我相信 A 先生離職，是要追求更有挑戰性的工作機會。

注意事項：

(1)本文全部例句裡所指的人、性別和動詞時態，都可改變。被推薦人如已離職，動詞則用過去式。

(2)推薦信屬正式信件，所以少用俚語或口語。

(3)通常只寫被推薦者的優點和積極性，而不寫缺點，以免影響其前途。

(4)不可過分吹噓，以免減低真實性和可信度。即使被推薦者的優點很多，也只要集中幾個要點。

(5)對被推薦者的能力，不可因私人的偏見而影響公正性。

(6)用「To Whom It May Concern」（敬啟者）開頭的公開推薦信，通常效力較差，最好知道負責人的名字和職位。

Chapter 6

老美抱怨／
批評的說法

老美抱怨／批評的說法

　　一般老美會克制自己，不願在別人面前抱怨、批評或發牢騷，因為他們要維護形象和表現修養，也避免被人冠上「低品格」或「牢騷鬼」的惡名。

　　以下是老美對抱怨或批評的一些說法。在用字和語氣上，也較含蓄和文明，洋味十足，可算是道地的英文。

　　這裡我把埋怨與批評，分為對人、對事和特別情況三方面來說。（句中的主詞、人稱、單複數、時態都可改變）

1. 對人的埋怨或批評

He is unkind and selfish, thinking only of himself.

他不仁慈，很自私，只為自己著想。

Bob appears to be a constant downer.

Bob 看來是個總是說喪氣話的人。

（downer＝someone often talks negative things）

Mr. A has run many friends off with his negativity.

A 先生的消極態度，讓許多朋友避而遠之。

（to run someone off 使人逃走）

He needs something to keep his head on straight.

他需要某些東西讓他思維清醒些。

（to keep one's head on straight＝think clearly）

Mr. B always steps out of line in his remarks.

B 先生所做的評論，常常不得體。

（to step out of line 不合時宜＝say or act inappropriately）

He is a cruel, ruthless man and his wife has cried a bucket of tears.

他是位殘忍無情的人，他太太已哭得淚如傾瀉。

（bucket 水桶）

It seems that she has just been on an emotional roller coaster.

她似乎在情緒上忽好忽壞，大起大落。

（roller coaster 是遊樂場的雲霄飛車）

She complains that Mr. A is rude, vulgar and makes constant sexual innuendos.

她抱怨 A 先生粗魯不雅，常常做出性暗示。

（innuendo 是影射或暗示）

He is impossible to talk to; he is becoming increasingly difficult to work with.

人們無法與他溝通，也越來越難和他共事。

His ego must be huge while his common sense is nil.

他很自大，但沒有常識。

（ego 的複數是 egos；nil＝zero）

At the ripe old age of 30, he has become a know-it-all.

他剛滿 30 歲，就自以為無所不知。

（at the ripe old age 是諷刺語，意謂「剛滿」多少歲，就自認超人聰明。＝ smart aleck＝smart alick，但實際不是那麼一回事。know-it-all＝know-all 也是諷刺的口語，因為世上哪有「無所不知」的「超人」呢？）

On this matter, Mr. B is way off base.

對這件事，B 先生是大錯特錯

（way off base＝far off the mark 也就是 seriously wrong）

He is really rubbing me the wrong way; I feel stabbed in the back.

他真令我惱火；我感到背後被捅一刀。

（to rub someone (up) the wrong way 惹怒某人；to stab in the back 暗中傷人，背地中傷或捅人一刀。）

Bitterness, and name-calling have been the hallmark of relations between them.

怨恨和辱罵已成為他們關係的特徵。

（hallmark 是標記或特徵＝distinguishing figure）

His affair with his ex-wife has ticked his wife off.

他和前妻有染，讓他太太發火。

（to tick someone off＝to make someone mad）

She is at the end of her rope; she has nowhere to turn to escape.

她是智窮力竭，走投無路。

（at the end of one's rope 是山窮水盡，智窮力竭＝no choice; no any alternative，前面的動詞用 to be 或 come 或 get）

Not to round shallow, Mr. B is not as honest as you think.

我不是貶低他，B 先生不是你認為的那麼誠實。

（shallow 本是膚淺，乏味。Not to round shallow 多半指輕微的批評＝not really to put him down）

He always criticizes his children in a scolding tone.

他老是用責罵的口氣批評他的孩子。

Being hateful, self-centered and a user of other people, he has few friends.

他有憎恨、自私和利用他人的本性，所以幾乎沒有朋友。

（self-centered 自我中心＝selfish）

Every time they talked, they just did not see eye to eye.

他們每次相談就是無法意見相同。

（see eye to eye＝agree）

He is a pathological liar; nothing of what he brags about is true.

他是一位病態的撒謊者；他所吹噓的全是假的。

（pathological liar 是種天性或有病的撒謊者，也就是 natural liar 或 born liar）

If he doesn't get his way, he throws a temper tantrum like a five-year-old does.

如果不照他的意思，他就像五歲孩子那樣大發脾氣。

（to get one's [own] way 照個人的意思行事；temper 指情緒或怒氣；tantrum 是發脾氣；to throw a temper tantrum 特別指像小孩一樣容易發脾氣。）

He is a real control freak, but his wife is blind about it.

他是一位控制狂，但他太太不甩他。

（freak 本是怪物、反常；control freak＝someone who is over-controlling; to be blind about something＝to ignore something）

As a constant complainer, John drags us down in the dumps.

John 是個不斷抱怨的「牢騷鬼」，把我們拉入負面情緒。

（drag 是拖、拉；時態：dragged, dragging; dumps 是沮喪，但單數 dump 是垃圾堆。）(down in the dumps 悶悶不樂；to drag someone down in the dumps ＝to make someone have negative feelings.）

Unfortunately, Mr. A continues to treat his wife like a doormat.

不幸地，A 先生繼續把他太太當腳踏墊踐踏。

（doormat＝a piece of dirt；也可解為「出氣筒」）

When Mr. B gets mad at his wife, it turns into a screaming match.

當 B 先生對他太太發怒時，情況就變成互相大叫。

（screaming match＝scream at each other）

He often lashes out at his son over minor things.

他常常為了小事，嚴詞責罵他的兒子。

(lash 本是嚴責；to lash out at someone 是對某人生氣，責罵＝get angry at someone)

Bob is clumsy and heavy-handed, sort of a bull in a china shop.

Bob 笨手笨腳，是有點粗魯、容易闖禍的人。

(clumsy and heavy-handed 指笨手笨腳，容易打破東西＝break things easily; a bull in a china shop 本指公牛在瓷器店鋪裡，容易闖禍＝may make things worse)

With his explosive temper, World War III would erupt right here if she did this to him.

以他暴躁的脾氣，假如她對他做了這件事，第三次世界大戰將會在此爆發。

It seems she has married someone who is a little rough around the edges.

她似乎嫁給一個舉止粗魯的人。

(rough around the edges＝not well-mannered)

Mr. A is argumentative so he created a lot of family drama.

A 先生很愛爭辯，引起家庭許多的爭吵。

(family drama＝argument)

She is unorganized and sometimes it spills over into her life.

她是雜亂無章，沒條理的人，有時影響到她的生活。

（it 指她雜亂無章這件事；spill over 本是散落或流到。spill 的時態：spilt 或 spilled, spilling）

He picks up and drops hobbies in the span of weeks; what can he do to find his niche?

他幾星期內，嘗試放棄多項興趣；這樣三心二意，他要做什麼才能找到專長領域呢？

（in the span of＝within; niche＝suitable job or hobby）

Bob is out of line to ask his girlfriend to split the bills in half.

Bob 要他女友付一半的帳，很不合理。

（out of line＝unreasonable）

He is so vested in his bias that it is unlikely he will change.

他的偏見，根深柢固，很難改變。

（vested 本是隸屬或給予＝devote it so much; locked in）

Bob has been secretive and domineering; he sometimes raises Cain in front of the kids.

Bob 一向是遮遮掩掩，作威作福，有時還在孩子面前大發雷霆。

（secretive 是不坦率，遮遮掩掩；domineering 是盛氣凌人；raise Cain 是大發脾氣。Cain 是來自聖經創世紀，本指亞當與夏娃的長子，殺其弟亞伯，後人尤指殺兄弟者。C 要大寫）

People who are unhappy with themselves sometimes take it out on others.

有些人自己不高興，就在別人頭上發洩。

(it 指自己不高興的事)

That he took out his frustrations on his wife is despicable.

他自己受挫，發洩在他太太頭上，很卑鄙。

(frustration 指挫折或怒氣；to take out something on someone 向某人發洩怨氣。)

He uses his position of power to sexually harass his female employees.

他利用職權，對女職員性騷擾。

He seems to hold grudges over the stupidest things.

他似乎為無聊小事而尋求報復。

(to hold grudges＝to seek revenge)

Bob considers his step-son to be nothing more than excess baggage.

Bob 認為他的繼子只是多餘的包袱。

(excess baggage 本指超重行李，這裡是 unnecessary burden)

Being a sham, a hypocrite and a fraud, he is not trustworthy.

他是個虛偽、偽善的騙子，並不值得信任。

(sham 就是 fake; fraud 也是 liar; hypocrite 就是 say one thing and do the other)

She loves him dearly, but she always feels like she is no.2, 3 or 4 in his life.

她很愛他，但她總覺得她在他生命中，只是二、三或四號人物。

This young stay-at-home mother's fuse is getting shorter every day.

這位不上班在家的年輕母親，每天脾氣愈來愈大。

（getting shorter fuse＝having short temper）

He can't figure out why on earth she is angry at him.

他想不出到底為什麼她生他的氣。

（on earth 是到底或究竟；一般用在疑問句表示加強語氣＝in any way）

Mrs. A is wary of her boy with his loud foul mouth.

A 太太對大聲說髒話的兒子提高警覺。

（wary 是小心翼翼，提高警覺；foul mouth 說髒話＝vulgar language）

This young man is at his wit's end dealing with his father.

這位年輕人全然不知如何與父親相處。

（wit 本是風趣；at one's wit's end 是智窮計盡，束手無策＝use up all ideas）

He may not realize how offensive his bickering and name-calling are to others.

他也許不能體會他的爭吵和辱罵對別人有多大傷害。

（bicker 爭吵＝argue; name-calling 辱罵，當名詞）

She never lifted a finger to do dishes, clean her room or even prepare a meal for herself.

她從不幫忙洗碗、清理房間或為自己準備一餐飯。

(to lift a finger 舉手之勞或幫點忙；to do dishes＝to wash dishes)

Bob is doomed to be a Jack of all trades and will never stick with a job longer than 6 months.

Bob 注定是位雜而不精的人，他很難保住工作超過半年。

(doom 是命定或注定；Jack of all trades 原本後面有「and master of none」，但多半省去，此句指做每種工作都不求精)

His 30-year-old druggie doesn't work and sponges off his mom by making promises he never keeps.

30 歲的毒蟲不工作，靠母親養活，總作沒實現的承諾。

(druggie 吸毒者；to sponge off someone 靠某人吃喝)

He is putting his wife down under the guise of humor.

他在幽默的幌子下，貶低太太。

(to put someone down 是奚落、貶低)

She still stays in touch with him, but her heart is no longer where it was.

她仍然與他保持聯絡，不過她的心不再與過去一樣。

(to stay in touch with someone 與某人保持聯絡)

Really, she was hurt to the core in this matter.

的確，這件事深深地傷了他的心。

(hurt to the core＝deeply or completely hurt)

This is his attempt to put a wedge between them.

這是他試圖挑起他們之間的不和。

(wedge 是障礙或隔閡＝barrier)

He is not usually sarcastic, but this is a pretty strange remark.

他通常不太挖苦人，但這是一個特別奇怪的評論。

(sarcastic 是嘲笑、諷刺；名詞是 sarcasm)

Bob appears to be both vindictive and extortionate.

他顯出一副要報復和敲詐的樣子。

(extortionate 是勒索的，敲詐的；extortion 是名詞)

It's always someone else's fault if something goes wrong with him.

他假如有什麼事出錯，那都是別人的錯。

He is always uptight; he doesn't roll with the punches well.

他常常煩躁不安，無法與人和諧相處。

(roll with the punches＝get along with others)

He seems to feel (that) his pain is her gain.

他覺得他的痛苦，是她的收獲。

2. 對事物的埋怨或批評：

Face to face communication is a lost skill for the younger generation.

年輕一代，喪失了面對面的溝通技能。

The signals that people send through facial expressions and gestures are being lost because of over-dependence on high technology.

由於過分依賴高科技，人們經由表情和動作示意的訊息，正在消失。

Online dating can't always cure loneliness.

網路約會未必能解決寂寞之苦。

Eavesdropping is a very unpleasant trait; in the interest of harmony it should be cut out.

竊聽是件令人不愉快的事，為了和諧相處，應該停止。

（eavesdrop 是動詞，竊聽之意；to be cut out＝to be stopped）

The latest uproar in his family is much ado about nothing.

他家最近的爭端只是芝麻小事，毫無意義。

（ado 是紛擾或麻煩；much ado about（或 over）nothing 是無事生非，沒有意義的小事＝trivial or meaningless）

也可加上其他字眼：

The whole controversy is far too much ado about absolutely nothing.

整個爭議完全是無事生非。

Her day-in and day-out misery comes from her husband.

她日復一日的痛苦，都是來自她的老公。

（day-in and day-out＝continuing）

What he is doing keeps annoying me like a mosquito buzzing in my ears or a pebble stuck in my shoes.

他所做的讓我厭煩，就像一隻蚊子在耳邊嗡嗡叫，或像一塊卡在鞋裡的小石頭。

（annoy 是惱怒；buzz 是嗡嗡聲；stick 是塞在或卡住；過去式和過去分詞是 stuck 或 sticked）

Verbal abuse is as bad as physical one. The scars heal, but the words keep playing over and over like a tape in your head.

口語辱罵和肉體摧殘同樣糟，傷痕可以結疤痊癒，但辱罵就像錄音帶在你腦子裡反覆播放。

（注意：scar 是「傷痕」，不同於 scare「恐懼」）

To put it bluntly, what he did gives me the creeps.

老實說，他的所作所為令我嘔心。

（to put it bluntly＝truthfully＝speak in truthful manner＝frankly speaking）

Discipline is not what you do to someone; it's what you do for someone.

紀律規章不是對他人做什麼，而是為他人做什麼。

(to someone＝against someone; for someone＝on someone's behalf 或 for someone's own good)

(The) guilt and regret are eating her alive.

內疚和遺憾，令她非常苦惱。

(to eat someone alive＝to make someone very upset；句前如加定冠詞 the，表示特別情況的內疚)

Not everything you read online is the gospel truth.

你在網路上所看到的，未必都是事實。

(gospel truth＝complete truth; really true)

Taking care of his elderly mother would take a heavy toll on his finances.

照顧年老的母親，對他的財力將造成重大的影響。

(to take a (或 its) toll 造成危害；to take a heavy toll on something 是對某事造成重大的損害，elderly 指上了年紀的，是對長者較尊敬的稱呼。)

Mr. Wang's comments hit her like a ton of bricks.

王先生的評論給她打擊很大。

(a ton of bricks 一噸的磚塊，在此表示很重的東西)

She definitely does not fit in with her American husband's family; she often feels disregarded.

她確實無法適應她美國老公的家庭；她常覺得不受尊重。

(to fit in 是適應＝to get along or to match)

Family issues seem to have been (或 to be) the recurring theme of her life.

家庭爭議似乎是她生活上反覆出現的主題。

(recur 反覆出現，時態是 recurred, recurring; recurring theme＝same problem over and over again)

His actions appear to be fake, attention-getting, goofy and childish.

他的舉止顯然是假裝的，想獲得別人注意，愚蠢和幼稚。

(attention-getting＝attention greedy＝to get attention; goofy＝a little bit crazy)

In fighting and personal attacks among many Chinese have taken their toll.

許多老中的內部暗鬥和人身攻擊，造成自身損害。

One thing leading to another has made her break into tears.

事情接二連三，使她淚流滿面。

(注意，一般不說：has broken her into tears)

This matter is really eating away at her and is eating her husband up inside, too.

這件事真使她煩惱，也使她老公內心焦慮。

(to eat away at someone 使某人煩惱＝to upset someone; to eat someone up 使某人焦慮＝to bother someone)

On this touchy issue, she should listen to her head rather than go with her heart.

在這敏感的議題上，她應該理智分析，不要感情用事。

(to listen to one's head＝to think logically; to go with one's heart＝to be emotional)

Many credit card holders' hearts outweighed their heads on shopping sprees.

許多信用卡持卡人，在狂熱購買的行為裡，感情超過理智的比重。

(outweigh 是超過……比重；spree 是狂熱行為)

也可說成：Many credit card holders let their hearts do shopping rather than their heads.

It seems that Americans dream no small dreams and spend no small amounts.

美國人似乎做不小的夢，也花不少的錢。

(第一個 dream 是動詞；第二個 dreams 是名詞；amounts 後面省去 of money)

Isolationism and protectionism could worsen the financial crisis.

(政治或經濟的)孤立主義和保護主義，都可能使金融危機更加惡化。

(crisis 危機；複數是 crises)

The outlook for inflation is uncertain and the president doesn't have a magic wand.

通貨膨脹的前景難以預料，總統也無魔杖可施。

There seems no end in sight to the woes of the housing industry and (the) mortgage market.

房地產和借貸業的困境，似乎在短期內無法終止。

(woe 困難＝trouble; no end in sight＝no immediate end)

His casual work ethic angers his diligent colleagues.

他漫不經心的工作德性，令勤奮的同事們生氣。

If his sex scandal is brought to light, it will hit him below the belt.

如果他的緋聞被抖出來，他就會自取其辱。

(to bring to light 揭露＝to reveal；也可用被動 to be brought to light; hit below the belt 指不按規律行事，侮辱了自己。)

Their relationship is going nowhere positive and she should give that heel the boot.

他們的關係毫無良性進展，她應該把那位壞傢伙休掉。

(在這裡，heel 和 boot 都是俚語；heel 是指卑鄙可惡的人＝bad person; boot 本是靴子，這裡是踢出去或逐出去＝kick him out 或 get rid of him)

Staff infighting, backbiting and the like seem to be the rule rather than the exception.

員工的內部暗鬥，及誹謗和類似事情，似乎成了習慣，而非例外。

(動詞時態：infight, infought, infought, infighting；backbite, backbit, backbitten, backbiting)

What he has been trying is to play both ends against the middle.

他的所做所為，就是設法使雙方相爭，而他從中得利。

Why change anything when things are pretty great / good right now?

現在一切都很好，為何要改變呢？

A nice and honest person often gets a short end of stick.

誠實的好人常常受到不公平的待遇。(好人受欺)

(to get a / the short / dirty end of stick 是受到不公平待遇)

His intentional invasion of her space really upset his girlfriend.

他有意侵犯她的個人空間，使他的女友惱火。

(to invade someone's space 就是站得太近，把別人的空間佔去＝to be too close)

Uncle Sam is running in the red and has been for a long time.

美國政府長期以來，一直都是負債累累。

(in the red＝in debt or in deficit; has been 後面省去了 in the red)

(An economic) recession or not, call it what you like, it's belt-tightening time.

經濟蕭條與否，隨你怎麼說，這是勒緊褲帶的時候了。

(to tighten one's belt 省吃儉用)

Clobbered by pink slips, shrinking nest eggs and falling home values, we are holding even tighter to our wallets.

由於遭到解僱、存款減少和房價滑落的衝擊，我們更要看緊錢包。

(pink slip「粉紅單」，是解僱通知單；nest egg 暱稱儲蓄或存款；clobber 遭到……打擊；to hold tighter to one's wallet＝to spend less money)

Our paychecks and nest eggs are taking a hit.

我們的薪水和積蓄受到打擊愈來愈少。

(to take a hit＝to suffer a lose or to be reduced)

His tall tales should make him blush with shame.

他的無稽之談應該要使他難為情。

(tall tale＝tall story 無稽之談＝exaggerating or bragging；blush with shame＝embarrassed)

Because of her actions, Bob feels a bewilderment and a sense of betrayal.

她的行為讓 Bob 感到迷惑和被背叛。

Photos posted online really irk some people who prefer privacy.

放在網路上的照片，實在讓一些想要隱私的人厭煩。

(irk 使厭煩)

 特別情況的埋怨或訴求

　　這通常用在書面上，因較正式，故少用俚語或口語。(下面的例句，也可組成一封短信)

1. 抱怨鄰居放狗：

The is the third time I saw your dog in my yard. My wife continues to be frightened by the dogs.

這是我第三次看到你的狗在我的院子裡。我太太仍然被你的狗嚇到。

There have been several reports of dog biting or snapping at people.

有幾次狗咬人或猛抓人的報導。

動詞時態：

bite, bit, bitten, biting（不是 bitting）, snap, snapped, snapping

I would like to come to some kind of agreement without hurting each other's feelings.

我希望能達成某種協議，也不傷害彼此感情。

2. 埋怨鄰居太吵：

We have been renting your apartment for the past three years and have been pleased with our situation until just recently when new tenants moved into the next apartment.

我們租你的公寓已三年，並且對情況很滿意，直到最近新房客搬來隔壁為止。

Having spoken to the new tenants about their frequent parties, high musical volume and loud noise after 11 p.m., we have not received any favorable response.

我們也跟新房客談過有關他們在晚上 11 點後頻繁的派對，以及高聲的音樂和嘈雜，但我們還未得到任何合宜的回答。

Your cooperation will be appreciated.

你的合作將受感激。

3. 埋怨店員無禮：

I would like to let you know that your employee Mr. A was very rude to me when I was in your store last week.

我想讓你知道，上周我在你的店鋪時，你的員工 A 先生對我很不禮貌。

He answered my questions in a very loud voice.

他大聲地回答我的問題。

By making fun of my English accent, he used some sarcastic words in an exaggerated fashion.

他取笑我的英語口音，並以誇張的形式使用嘲笑的字眼。

Even if I had as little command of the English language as Mr. A assumed, I feel he should treat every customer with respect.

即使我的英語像 A 先生想像中的差，我認為他對每一位顧客都要尊重。

I feel you are the right person to inform about this.

我想你是通知這件事的適當對象。

4. 抱怨保險沒有降價：

When I first bought my auto insurance from your company I was told that buying auto and homeowner insurance together from you would guarantee me a 10% rate reduction.

當我第一次向貴公司購買汽車保險時，你們告訴我，如果我自貴公司合買汽車和房屋保險，則保證有百分之十的減價。

But I find I am paying substantially the same as I paid separately before.

但我目前所付的錢，實際上與過去分開付時一樣。

I would appreciate it if you please check to see why I am not getting the lower rate.

如果你能查詢為何我沒有取得較低價格，我會很感謝。

5. 貨品沒有打折：

I received your invoice #201, dated March 10, 2011, for a computer I bought at the price of $800.

我購買一台 800 元的電腦，你寄來的發貨單第 201 號日期是 2011 年 3 月 10 日已經收到。

It was my understanding that the computer would be billed at 20% sale discount.

據我所知，該電腦價格應有百分二十的減價。

I should appreciate it if you send me a new bill in the right amount.

如果你能寄來一份數目正確的新帳單，我會很感謝。

6. 貨品不符規格：

I ordered two men's shirts, invoice #110, which arrived yesterday.

我昨天收到訂購的兩件男士襯衫，發票號碼為 110 號。

Unfortunately, the color and the quality are not up to my specifications.

遺憾的是，襯衫的顏色和品質不是我所要的規格。

I am returning the shirts and expect to receive the correct merchandise or a full refund at your earliest convenience.

我把襯衫退回，並希望盡早收到符合規格的貨品或者全額退款。

7. 傢俱品質不良：

On January 10, 2012, I bought a sofa from your company with a one year warranty.

2012 年 1 月 10 號，我自貴公司買了一張保固一年的沙發。

After we have used it for a month, the springs are starting to drop down.

我們使用一個月後，彈簧開始下垂。

I would like to return the sofa to you for a replacement with one that lives up to its price tag or receive a full refund.

我想把沙發退還給你，換一張水準符合標籤上價格的沙發，或且收到全額退款。

Please contact me upon your receipt of this letter.

收到此信後，請與我聯絡。

8. 品質不良而退貨：

I have just received the jacket I ordered with your invoice #202.

我剛收到我訂購的夾克，發票號碼是 202 號。

Unfortunately, this is not exactly the merchandise shown in your catalog. The quality does not measure up to your advertised jacket, either.

遺憾的是，這不符合目錄上顯示的產品。品質與廣告裡描述的夾克也有差異。

I am returning the jacket by u.p.s. Please credit my account in full.

現在我用 u.p.s 退還這件夾克，請在我的帳戶裡記入全額。

(u.p.s. = united parcel service)

9. 貨物遲到：

My purchase for an electric massager, order #101, dated March 10, 2011, up to now, has not arrived.

我於 2011 年 3 月 10 日訂購一件電動按摩器，訂單號碼 101，至今尚未到達。

I shall appreciate your letting me know exactly how this matter stands. You may reach me at XXX-XXX-XXXX.

這件事的真正情形如何，請與我聯絡。我的電話是 XXX-XXX-XXXX。

10. 催促來貨：

May I call your attention to my purchase order #201, dated March 3, 2011. I cannot understand why the item I ordered has been delayed so long.

敬請注意我 2011 年 3 月 3 日第 201 號訂單。我不了解為何我所訂購的項目會耽擱這麼久。

As this is a seasonal item, it's important for me to receive it as soon as possible.

由於這是項有季節性的東西，能夠盡快收到對我很重要。

另一個例子：

On March 5, 2011, I placed an order for a man's leather jacket, but up to now, I have not received the merchandise.

2011 年 3 月 5 日，我訂購一件男裝皮夾克，至今還未收到。

Please advise me when I can expect to receive it.

何時才能收到，請告知。

As my order #121 of March 10, 2011, for a power juicer has been delayed for so long. I am hereby canceling my order.

由於我 2011 年 3 月 10 日訂購一台強力果汁機，訂單號碼 121 號，已耽擱很久，在此我要取消這項訂單。

11. 來貨不全：

On Feb. 10, 2011, I ordered from your company two jackets, three shirts and two men's belts.

2011 年 2 月 10 日我向貴公司訂購兩件夾克，三件襯衫和兩條男裝皮帶。

So far I have received everything except two belts. Please let me know what happened to the belts.

至今除兩條皮帶外，其他都已收到。請告訴我皮帶是怎麼回事？

或類似情況：

With your invoice #202, I regret to inform you a shortage in the package you sent me by u.p.s.

你用 u.p.s. 寄來的包裹裡，照發票第 202 號所列，很遺憾，缺了東西。

Please send me one more pair of shoes I ordered.

請再寄給我一雙我所訂購的鞋子。

12. 帳單錯誤：

On March 15, 2011, I purchased and charged to my account a portable TV at the price of $250 and I returned it to your company on the same day because of a defect.

2011 年 3 月 15 日，我賒購一台 250 元的手提電視機，由於瑕疵，我當天退還給貴公司。

I am still being billed every month since then.

自從那天起，你們每月還是寄來帳單。

My several letters to your billing department have had no results.

我寫了幾封信給你們的清帳部門，毫無結果。

Please put a stop to this incorrect billing in my name. If you ignore this, I will have to think about legal action.

請停止以我的名字開出這種錯誤的帳單。假如你們對這件事置之不理，我必須考慮採取法律行動。

　　註：也可說成 I'll have to ask my lawyer to handle this. 或 I'll leave this to my attorney.

　　表示由律師處理，但不必使用威脅性的字眼。

　　類似的錯誤帳單：

As your 20-year customer, I'm making this first-time letter of complaint.

做為你廿年的顧客，我第一次寫這封抱怨信。

Your service man has already picked up the defective refrigerator last month and I assume he returned it to your company.

上個月你的服務員已取走那台有問題的冰箱，我設想他已把冰箱送回貴公司。

Please stop billing me or I may have to report this matter to the Better Business Bureau.

請停止給我帳單，否則我會把這件事向商業改善局報告。

　　註：也叫「三 B」(Triple B)是美國商業投訴的機關。商人為了信譽，也不願見到顧客投訴。

　　另一錯誤的帳單：

Your March statement, 2011, on my acount appears to be incorrect.

你寄來 2011 年三月份的結算單，我的戶頭顯然有錯。

The previous balance was only $152, but the current statement shows this balance as $1152.

上次的餘額是 152 元，但現在的結算單卻是 1152 元。

As soon as I receive your revised bill, I will send you a check in full.

一旦我收到你修正後的帳單，我會寄上支票全數付清。

(13)電費太貴：

I have made an adjustment claim for my over-charged electric bill in January 2011, but nothing has been done to it.

我對 2011 年元月份的電費超額收費做出調整的要求，但沒有任何動靜。

I am holding up the payment of my bill pending the settlement of this matter.

我暫時不付這筆錢，等待這件事解決。

Should your company make no move to verify my claim, it may be necessary to ask Public Utility Commission to resolve the problem.

假如貴公司不查清我的要求，我也許必須請公共水電督察委員會解決這個問題。

14. 請求餐館賠償：

As your well-satisfied patron for years, I hate to send you this letter.

由於我是你們多年來滿意的顧客，我真不願寄這封信給你。

Last week when I was dining at your restaurant, your server accidentally tipped the soup and spilled it over my new suit.

上周我在你們的餐館吃飯時，你們的服務員不慎弄翻湯、把湯灑在我的新衣上。

I assured the server (that) the cleaners would remove the spot, and that is why I did not report to you at that time.

我叫服務員放心，洗衣店可以去掉汙漬。這是我那時沒有告訴你的原因。

Now that the spot cannot be removed, I wonder if the damage to my suit can be compensated.

然而現在汙漬去不掉，我不知可否請求衣服損害的補償。

I would appreciate your prompt attention to this matter.

如蒙迅速回音，則十分感謝。

註：spill（不小心）溢出；時態：spilt 或 spilled, spilling；tip 翻倒；時態：tipped, tipping

一般餐館的 waiter（男侍者）和 waitress（女侍者）現在統稱為 server。

Chapter 7

老美婉拒／
解窘的說法

　　老外重視人際關係（interpersonal relation），以免傷害別人的感情。遇到不願意接受別人的邀請或要求時，也用「圓融」「得體」（tactful）的方式，加以推辭或婉拒（decline or refusal），有時也用「白謊」（white lie）為藉口，因為他們認為白謊，無傷大雅，既不傷害感情，還可保持友誼。

　　此外，老外遇到尷尬或出醜時，也能藉故迴避，或輕鬆地自我解窘。

　　這裡我用不同的句型，分幾方面來說。希望能對一些「不技巧」（tactless）的老中，有「舉一反三」、「取長補短」的好處。（句中的主詞、單複數、動詞時態或邀請的場合，均可改變）

婉拒邀請（Declining an invitation）

　　這包括親友的生日、婚禮或其他場口的邀請，不論是藉口或是事實，你可在口頭上、或在卡片或短信上，客氣地寫上幾個婉拒的字句。

　　例如：

I would love to attend your party, but I have a previous engagement.
我真想要參加你的宴會，但我事前已經有約。

I would be very happy to go with you, but I have to do something else tonight.

我本來真高興能與你同去,可是我今晚必須要做其他的事。

I'm unable to be with you for your birthday party because I'll be out of town on that day.

我不能參加你的生日會,因為那天我要出城。

Please accept my sincere regret for not being able to join you.

不能參加,請接受我至誠的歉意。

I regret having to miss your birthday party, I shall be (away) on my vacation at that time.

抱歉,我必須錯過你的生日會,那天我正好離開前往度假。

I regret that I'm unable to accept your kind invitation because of a previous appointment. I know I'll be missing a wonderful time.

由於事先有約,我不能接受你的邀請,感到抱歉,我知道我將錯過一個難得的日子。

Unfortunately, you have caught me at the wrong time. I am over-scheduled for the next two weeks.

真遺憾,你找錯了時間,我下兩周的行程已經排得滿滿的。

I am sorry for not being able to attend the meeting at that time, but I'm free the following week.

對不起,我不能參加那天的會議:不過隔周,我就有空。

My present schedule is regrettably very inflexible. I hope you'll give me a rain check.

很遺憾我目前的行程無法更改，我希望你能改日再度邀請。

I am sorry I am not able to reschedule my previous commitment for that day. Thank you for thinking of me.

真抱歉，那天我不能改變事先已安排的承諾。謝謝你想到我。

It is a disappointment to miss not only your birthday party but also the opportunity to meet you and your other friends.

令人失望的，不但是錯過你的生日會，也不能見到你和你的其他朋友。

I regretfully inform you that my wife and I will have to be out of town on the night of your wedding day and that we shall have to decline your kind invitation.

真對不起，你結婚那天晚上，內人和我都將遠行出城，所以必須婉謝你的親切邀請。

My wife and I regret that, because of a previous engagement, we are unable to accept your invitation for Sunday, the second of May at 6 p.m.

由於事先有約，內人和我感到抱歉，不能參加你 5 月 2 日星期天下午 6 點的邀請。

Thank you for your letter inviting me to your home for a weekend get-together. As I am going to attend my friend's graduation that weekend, I'll have to say no this time.

謝謝來信邀請我到府上參加周末的歡聚。由於那個周末我要參加朋友的畢業典禮，這回只好說不。

I must unfortunately decline to participate in your fund-raising party next weekend. I'll try to go another time.

很遺憾，我無法參加你下周末的募款宴會，下回我再設法參加。

I very much regret that because of a previously scheduled engagement I will not be able to join you for dinner next Saturday. May I have a rain check?

因為事前安排好的約會，我為無法參加你下周六的晚餐感到非常抱歉。你能再次邀請我嗎？

Thanks so much for your invitation to be your guest over the weekend of May third. You know how much I'd love to accept, but I'll have to say no this time because of a previous commitment.

非常謝謝你邀請我作為你 5 月 3 日周末的客人。你知道我多麼想去，但這次因為事先有約，我必須說不。

It's with disappointment that I have to say that I shall be unable to attend your wedding on May 10 because I have to attend a meeting in New York at that time. Thank you for including me among your friends.

真令人失望的是我不能參加你 5 月 10 日的婚禮，因為那天我必須去紐約開會。謝謝你把我包括在你的朋友之中。

What a shame! I won't be able to accept your invitation to a weekend get-together party for May 10. Thank you for thinking of me and making me a tempting offer.

真不巧，我無法前往你 5 月 10 日的周末歡聚。謝謝你想到我，給我一個誘人的邀請。

We would be with you at your graduation if it were not such a long distance between your town and ours.

要不是因為我們兩個城市相距這麼遠，我們就會參加你的畢業典禮。

Lilly and I regret exceedingly that we are unable to accept your invitation for dinner on Saturday May 10 as we have another engagement for that evening.

莉莉和我十分抱歉無法前往你 5 月 10 日星期六的晚餐邀請，因為那天晚上已經有另一約會。

I don't know how to tell you, John, but I won't be able to attend your wedding. Under such circumstance, I know you'll understand and forgive. I'll be with you in spirit.

John，我真不曉得怎樣告訴你，我無法參加你的婚禮。我知道在此情況下，你會理解和原諒。我的精神與你同在。

(I'll be with you in spirit. ＝ I'll be thinking of you.)

Thank you for your kind letter inviting us. We would enjoy seeing you again. However, we'll be out of town next week. So we'll have to say no this time.

謝謝來信邀請我們。本來我們會很高興再與你們相會，不過下周我們將要出城遠行，所以這次只好說不。

Nothing is more disappointing than having to turn down your invitation to your wedding anniversary party on Saturday, July 5. We are forced to do this because for that evening we have invited some friends to have dinner with us.

沒有什麼事比婉拒你們邀請參加 7 月 5 日周六的結婚周年紀念宴會更遺憾。我們這麼做是因為那天晚上我們已經請了幾位朋友一起吃飯。

I feel sorry that I shall not be able to join you for lunch on Saturday May 10. I have a doctor appointment that afternoon. Many thanks for asking me.

真對不起我不能參加你 5 月 10 日星期六的午餐。那天下午我和醫生有約。謝謝你的邀請。

We appreciate your attractive invitation to spend an evening at your home on July second. We can't think of a better way to spend an evening. Unfortunately, we have already accepted an invitation to our son's home. Therefore, it would be impossible for us to be there with you.

謝謝你們邀我們 7 月 2 日傍晚到府上作客,這邀請真吸引人。我們想不出度過一晚更好的方式。但很遺憾,我們已經答應兒子的邀請到他家去,所以不能與你們相聚。

We wish we could say yes to your kind invitation for your retirement gathering on April 10. We appreciate very much your inviting us.

我們真盼望能答應參加你們 4 月 10 日的退休聚會。我們感謝你的親切邀請。

Your pleasant invitation arrived today, and much as I regret it, I must decline. Lilly and I had already planned to spend next weekend with our daughter in Virginia. It would be so nice to see all of you. Thank you anyway.

你那真令人高興的邀請,今天收到。但真抱歉,我必須婉謝。因為內人和我已經計畫到維州女兒家度周末。如能見到你們大家該多好!不管如何,謝謝你。

(Much as I regret it, I must decline. ＝I sincerely regret that I must decline it.)

It's with real regret that I shall have to decline your invitation to attend the farewell party for Bob. Under separate mail, I am sending Bob a small gift. I wish him the best for everything in his future career.

真抱歉，我必須婉謝你邀請我參加 Bob 的送別會。我將給 Bob 另寄一件小禮物，我祝福他將來事業一帆風順。

I must say no very regretfully to your kind invitation. Unfortunately, there is uncertainty as to my husband's business travel plans. I don't feel it would be fair to you to delay a definite reply. Perhaps you'll be kind enough to repeat your invitation at some other time.

十分抱歉，我必須婉謝你親切的邀請。不料我先生的公務旅行計畫尚未確定。如果拖延給你確定的答覆，對你是不公平的。希望下次你能再度地親切邀請。

Thank you for asking me to speak at the multi-cultural event. I was honored to be asked to represent the Chinese community; however, I must decline this time. I would be glad to be of service on another occasion.

謝謝你邀請我在多元文化活動上演講。你請我代表華人社區，我感到十分榮幸。不過這次我必須婉謝，我願意在其他場合為你效勞。

Because of several other commitments, I'm unable to accept your invitation, but I'm sure you'll find a well-qualified speaker for this special occasion.

由於我其他幾個允諾，我無法領受你的邀請。不過我相信你能為這次的特別場合找到更勝任的演講人。

Thank you for inviting me to participate in the U.S.-China Friendship Conference. I'm flattered that you thought of me. Because of other commitments, I regret to say I'm unable to accept your invitation. I feel sure you'll find the right person for this meeting.

謝謝你邀請我參加中美友誼會議。你能想到我，感到榮幸。由於其他的允諾，很抱歉我無法赴會。不過我想你能找到合適的人參加這次會議。

婉拒協助的要求（Declining requests for assistance）

不能答應別人的請求時，老外也有簡單的方式婉拒。

例如：

I am sorry not to be able to assist you on this matter. I hope you can make other arrangements.

很抱歉這件事我無法幫忙，我希望你能想其他方法。

I sympathize with your request and (I) wish I could help.

我很體諒你的要求；我真盼望我能幫你。

I wish I could be more helpful, but it's just not possible right now.

我真盼望我能對你有所幫助，但目前沒有可能。

（I wish I could... 表示無能為力的假設語態）

Unfortunately, your request for assistance comes at a particularly difficult time for me.

真是不巧，你要求協助的時間，對我特別感到困難。

I appreciate your asking me to help with your problem. I hope I'll have the opportunity of saying yes at some other time.

謝謝你要我幫你解決問題，我希望下次我有機會能夠答應。

It's particularly difficult for me to turn down your request this time. Under other circumstances, I would be very happy to assist you.

這次婉拒你的要求，對我來說特別困難。不過在其他情況下，我會樂於協助。

I will see what I can do. You know I will try my best to assist you in whatever way possible. (或 possible way)

我會看看我能做什麼。你曉得我會在任何可能情況下幫你。

It's very difficult to say no to you as you can imagine, but I am not in a position to approve your proposal.

你能想像，對你說不十分困難，但以我的職責，無法批准你的提議。

Sorry, I am not in a position to do that for you; my hands are tied.

抱歉，以我的職位與立場，無能為力。

(my hands are tied＝beyond my power)

I am sorry I cannot help you at this time. I hope most sincerely that you may find another solution for this matter.

對不起，目前我不能幫你。我至誠的盼望你能找到其他解決此事的辦法。

I regret I cannot comply with your request. I would be glad to be of some assistance at another time.

我很抱歉無法順從你的要求。下次如有機會，當樂於效勞。

To be honest with you, this is not one of my talents. Is there anything else I could do for you?

老實說，這不是我的專長。有沒有其他的事，我能為你效勞？

Although the latest information you requested is not available, would this earlier report be suitable?

雖然你所要求的最新資料無法取得，這種之前的報告是否適用？

I am really sorry for not being able to say yes this time. Possibly I can be of some help to you at another time.

真抱歉，這次我不能答應你，也許下次我能有所效勞。

別人求職，無法幫忙，可以說：

We regret to say that our company is no longer considering applications for its computer programming positions.

很抱歉我們公司的電腦程式部門不再考慮聘請。

At this time there doesn't appear to be a position with us that is suited to your qualifications. However, I'll keep your resume on our active file.

目前我們似乎沒有適合你條件的職位，不過我把你的履歷表放在備查檔案中。

（active file 指隨時可以取用的檔案）

The position in our computer department for which you applied has been filled. We wish you good luck in your career. If any new opening occurs, we'll contact you.

閣下申請我們的電腦部門工作，該職缺已經填補，祝你事業順利。如有任何新的空缺，我會與你聯絡。

Thank you for the opportunity of considering your job application. Perhaps you could check back with us sometime next summer.

謝謝你給我考慮你申請工作的機會。也許明年暑假，你再與我連絡。

I am sorry to inform you that a careful consideration for your application does not indicate your suitability for the position. I wish you good luck in placing yourself elsewhere.

我很遺憾通知你，經過仔細審查你的申請後，顯示你不適合這個職位。祝福你在其他地方能找到工作。

（用 good luck 時，中間不加 of，但用 best of luck 時，中間要加 of）

After very careful considerations / deliberations, we have decided to offer the position to someone else. We'll contact you should a similar opening occur in the future. Best wishes in your seeking a challenging and rewarding position.

經過再三的考慮後，我們決定把這份工作提供給別人。他日有類似職缺時，我們再與你聯絡。祝福你找到一個挑戰性且有意義的工作。

（用 consideration 係指依各種條件為主的考慮，而 deliberation 是指含有爭議性的深思熟慮。）

　　或且，只謙虛地說：

Don't expect me to do this / to find you a job because I am just one little tiny piece of this organization.

不要指望我能幫上忙／能為你找到工作，我只是這個機構的一位小人物。

或：

I am just a cog in the wheel.

我只是輪子裡一個小螺絲釘而已。

一般老外熱心為慈善事業樂捐，但遇到財力不足時，也有婉拒的說法：

I certainly admire what you are doing for your (good) cause. I wish I could help you.

我的確很讚賞你為高尚目標而努力，我真希望能協助你。

As I am financially committed to some other charities, I am unable to send you anything. I hope you will understand.

由於我對其他慈善機構承諾經濟上的資助，我無法寄上任何東西。希望你能諒解。

Unfortunately, I am only able to make a one-time donation. Please accept my best wishes for success in your fund-raising.

遺憾的，我只能做一次性的樂捐。請接受我的祝福，願你募款成功。

As a retiree with a fixed income, I can only donate to our local community. Please take my name off your national mailing list.

我是靠固定收入的退休者，只能為我的社區樂捐。請在你們全國性的郵寄名單上，刪去我的名字。

也有老外不願在電話裡樂捐，以免詐騙，也會說：

I don't make donation on the phone. That is not the way I do things. Moreover, I have decided to donate only to our local charity / charities.

我不在電話裡樂捐，這不是我做事的方式；再說，我決定只捐給我們社區的慈善機構。

有時也會含蓄地說：

People are extremely sensitive about donated money / monies that is intended for one purpose being spent on another.

人們對某一種的捐款目標，而被用做其他用途時，特別敏感。(指有人把捐款作為私用)

(money 用複數 monies 時，指多筆、或來自多方的金錢。)

婉拒建議（Declining suggestions）

老外通常講求獨立、自主，不輕易接受他人的意見或建議，但也會婉轉的回拒。

例如：

You have a wonderful idea; may I think it over?

你的主意真好，可以讓我想想嗎？

That is really interesting; I never thought of it that way.

那真有趣，我從來沒那麼想過。

I respect your opinion, but I think there may be a better way to accomplish our project.

我尊重你的意見，但我想也許還有較好的方式來完成我們的計畫。

I can see your point and I will certainly think about it.

我了解你的觀點，我當會好好想想。

Your suggestion is valid, but let me think it over and I'll get back to you later.

你的建議很好，不過讓我想想，以後再通知你。

(valid＝good or useful)

As I am far from an expert on this, I certainly will give your opinion more thought.

對這件事，我不是專家，你的高見，我會好好考慮。

Your idea has merits, and I'll keep it in mind. Thank you for weighing in on this issue.

你的意見很有用，我會記在心裡。謝謝你參加這個議題。

(to weigh in＝to participate in)

I dislike throwing cold water on your opinion, but our current situation does not warrant accepting it.

我不喜歡在你的意見上潑冷水，但我們目前情況無法接受。

(warrant＝justify)

Although your suggestion is very appealing, our policy prohibits us from doing it.

雖然你的建議很有吸引力，但我們的政策不許這麼做。

Your idea is practical; let me check it out.

你的意見很實際，讓我再取得有關更多的資料。

(check it out＝get more information about it)

It is a wonderful program, but not a choice that I can make right now.

這是一個很棒的計畫，但不是我現在能做的選擇。

I certainly will give your proposal some thought to see how that would work out.

我對你的提議會好好的考慮，看看是否行得通。

I am sorry this one doesn't make the grade, but I hope your next proposal will be more successful.

抱歉，這個提案不能通過，但我希望下一個能成功。

(to make the grade＝to pass the grade)

Frankly speaking, I may have second thoughts about what you told me last time.

老實說，你上次所說的，我也許會再度考慮。

I can see your good points, but have you thought of our project another way?

我知道你有很好的主意，但你有沒有從另一角度衡量過我們的計畫？

Please tell me some more about your ideas and I will see what I can do.

請再告訴我一些你的想法，看看我能做些什麼。

While I cannot do much about this, I may suggest your idea to my boss.

這件事，我力有未逮，也許我能把你的高見向我老闆建議。

Really, I don't want to discourage you, but our budget-cut is a stumbling block.

真的，我不想讓你洩氣，但是我們的預算被砍，設下了障礙。

(stumbling block 本是絆腳石)

Maybe in the near future I may be able to use some of your idea. Anyway, I'll keep it in mind.

也許不久的將來，我能用上一些你的主意。不論怎樣，我會把它記在心裡。

Bob, I really appreciate your concern and efforts, but I must come to a decision in my own way.

Bob，我很感激你的關心和努力，但我必須以我自己的方法做出決定。

I respect your diagnosis about the problem, but I would like to get a second opinion.

我尊重你對這問題的判斷，不過我還要聽聽別的意見。

I don't think this will work for us. Good luck with selling your idea elsewhere.

我不認為這對我們行得通。願你的想法能用在別的地方。

We have had a chance to look at your proposal carefully, and we are sorry to say it is not right for us.

我們已經仔細地看過你的建議，但很遺憾不能適合我們。

婉拒回答問題（Declining to answer questions）

　　老外十分重視隱私權（privacy），對自己的年齡、薪水、貸款、體重等私事或有關敏感的問題，也常不做正面的回答。
　　例如：

Thank you for your interest, but I'd better not talk about it.

謝謝你的興趣，但我最好不談這件事。

At present, I feel this is a very sensitive issue. If you don't mind, I would rather not discuss it.

目前我覺得這是一件很敏感的事。你不介意的話，我倒不想談論。

I am not prepared to answer this question; I never thought about it.

我沒有準備回答這個問題；我從來沒有想到這件事。

How old do you think I am? Would you believe I am older than dirt?

你想我幾歲？你會相信我比泥土更老嗎？

I am old enough to know better than to tell you.

我年齡夠大，知道可以不必告訴你。

（表示我很懂事＝I am old enough not to tell you.）

My age is an unlisted number; you are close to be right.

我的年齡是不顯示號碼的。你說的很接近，大致不錯。

（an unlisted phone number 平時是指沒列在電話簿的電話號碼）

Fortunately, my salary has kept me off welfare（checks）.

僥倖，我的薪水讓我領不了社會福利金。

Well, so far my income has kept me out of the poorhouse.

噢，目前我的收入不會讓我身無分文。

(poorhouse 仍很常用＝being broke)

My mortgage is more than I intended to pay.

我的房貸付款，比我原先計畫的多些。

或：

I pay less / more than I thought I would.

我付出的比我想的少／多。

I weigh a little more than I wish I did.

我的體重比我所希望的多些。

遇到有人問你為何還不結婚，老外也會幽默地說：

I don't get married because I have never met a man / woman who deserved to be as happy as I could make him / her (to be happy).

我不結婚是因為我還沒遇到一位值得我讓他(她)無比幸福的男人(女人)

(to be happy 可省去)
也就是：I never met a man / woman who deserves to marry me; I am so wonderful.

Why should I marry and make one woman miserable, when I can remain single and make more women happy.

我為什麼要結婚而讓一位女人受罪，當我維持單身，能讓更多的女人高興。

(也就是：I should not get married.)

如果問到兒女的事，也可以說：

Gee, I really don't know. I never asked my son / daughter because I figured it was none of my business.

哎呀！我真不知道。我從未問過我兒子／女兒，因為我覺得那不關我的事。

(Gee 是 Jesus 或 God 的委婉語)

老外遇到「多管閒事」者，有時也會「不耐其煩」地說：

Why do you want to know how much I paid? Are you offering to make my next payment?

你為什麼要知道我付多少錢？難道你要為我付下一次的貸款嗎？

If it were any of your business, you would know about it.

假如這是你的事，你就會知道。

(言外之意是這不關你的事，所以你不必知道)

If you will forgive me for not answering, I will forgive you for asking.

假如你原諒我不回答，我也原諒你的發問。

This is a very personal question. How could that possibly concern you?

這是一個十分私人的問題，怎麼可能讓你關心呢？

What an incredibly rude question (it is); I cannot believe you asked that.

這是一個不可思議的粗魯問題，我不相信你竟然會發問。

不願男人常常「打擾」，老外女人也會「嚴正」地說：

I know we are old acquaintances, but I'm not interested in any kind of relationship with you. Please don't call me again.

我知道我們相識很久了，但我沒有興趣與你有任何的關係，請不要再打電話給我。

甚至更強調：

If you continue to bother me, I may have to speak to the police about a restraining order.

假如你繼續騷擾我，我也許會找警察，討論申請制止令。

（restraining order 是不准雙方來往的命令。）

老外多半不會「強求」或「死追」。男人聽到這些，也會「知難而退」，否則可能吃上「騷擾」的官司。

婉拒提供服務或產品（Declining offers of service or products）

遇到有人推銷新產品或某些特別服務，老外也會客氣的婉拒。

例如：

I appreciate your interest in me, but I don't feel that your service / product is one I need right now.

謝謝你對我的興趣，不過你所提供的服務／或產品，目前我不需要。

Even though your service seems very appealing, this is not something I am prepared to get at this time. I'll send this information to my friends who may be interested.

雖然你提供的服務，是蠻吸引人的，但不符合我現在所需。我可以把這個消息，轉告也許會有興趣的朋友。

It is possible that we would be interested in your service / product after this year.

也許明年我們對你的服務／產品有興趣。

I am really not interested in your service at this time. Perhaps you could check back with me next summer.

我現在實在對你的服務沒興趣，也許明年夏天你可再來找我。

We are very happy with what we have now. But you may give me your phone number in case I need to call you.

我們對現況很滿意，不過你可以給我電話號碼，如果需要時，我再與你聯絡。

It does not suit our needs at this time. This is not a priority for us, either.

目前這不適合我們的需要，也不是我們優先考慮的項目。

遇到慶祝場合，不要親友送禮時，也可婉辭：

You friendship / presence is a cherished / treasured gift and I respectfully request no other (gift).

你的友誼／光臨已經是一項珍貴的禮物，請不要再給我其他的禮物。

 ## 藉故逃避和自我紓困（**Making excuses and self justification**）

遇到「不耐煩」情況或尷尬場面，用來藉故開脫或自我辯解。

　　例如：

1. 某些場合，遇到有人與你喋喋不休，感到厭煩時，可藉口開脫：

Excuse me, I would like to say hi to our host.

抱歉，我想去向主人問個好。

My apologies! I have to talk to a friend whom I haven't seen in / for a while.

對不起，我要與一位很久不見的朋友聊聊。

(apologies＝many apologies)

Would you excuse me for a minute; I have to take a phone call.

請原諒，我要去接一通電話。

Well, I better go and mingle with some other people. It was nice talking to you.

哎呀！我最好與其他人交談一下。很高興能與你聊天。

　　三人交談時，要想開溜，可以說：

Two is company; three is a crowd. I am sure you two / both will have a lot to talk about.

兩人結伴，三人不歡。我相信你們兩位有很多話要談。

　　需要打斷別人發言的狀況下，可以說：

Sorry, John, we have to move on to the next item.

John，抱歉，我們必須討論下一個議題。

（用於開會有人喋喋不休時）

Well, Sir / Madam, you have made your points and I must move along. Thank you for calling.

噢！先生／夫人，你已經表達了你的立場，我還有其他事要做。謝謝你的電話。

（move along＝do something else）

Yes, you have said a mouthful. We can schedule another appointment at a time most convenient for you.

你所說的，已經包括很多了。我們可以再約一個你方便的時間。

（You have said a mouthful.＝You have covered more than I thought.＝What you said means a lot.）

藉故「開脫」的另外方式：

I am afraid I have held you too long.

我怕我已耽擱你很久了。

或 Am I holding you too long? I better let you go for now. I know your schedule is tight.

我現在讓你走吧！以後再談，我知道你的時程很緊湊。

（說 for now 表示 I will talk with you later）

I know you can do better yourself; I don't want to get in your way.

我知道，你自己會做得更好，我不想妨礙你。

（to get in one's way＝to be in the way 是妨礙）

We'll talk again when I have more time. Sorry, I have to cut our conversation short.

等我有較多的時間，我們再談吧！抱歉，我必須長話短說。

Why don't we set up an appointment for another day?

我們訂個時間，改天再談如何？

Thank you for coming in. Our talk has been very helpful. We must get together again sometime.

謝謝你來，我們的談話很有用，改天再聚吧！

其他「開脫」的場合與方式：

I really don't know, but I'll find it out and get back to you.

我真的不知道，不過我會打聽後再告訴你。

I will check on it and do whatever I can.

我要調查一下，盡力而為之。

I can't decide right now. Part of me think I should do this, and other part of me thinks I should not.

我現在不能決定。我一個想法是我應該做，另一個想法是我不該做。

（也就是：I can't make up my mind. Part of me thinks... and other part of me think... 是口語）

This is surely a pretty necklace; let me tell my wife about it.

這真是一條漂亮的項鍊，我會告訴內人。(不買東西的藉口)

I don't see I have any legal obligations in this regard.

我看不出我在這方面有任何法律義務上的束縛。

(不願被別人勉強做事時說)

Sorry, I am on medication which does not allow me to drink.

抱歉，我在服藥不能喝酒。

(這麼說，老外絕不會勉強叫你喝酒)

My doctor said I am not up to entertaining house guests this year. I'm sure you'll understand.

我的醫生說，今年不適合招待客人，我相信你能理解。

(也許是藉口)

I had hoped to visit you long ago, but one thing after another interfered with my plan.

我老早就想去拜訪你，但接二連三的事，影響了我的計畫。

(也許是藉口？)

If such a long distance did not separate us, I would be there in person for that special occasion.

要不是我們離得這麼遠，我會親自參加那個特別場合。

2. 遇到出醜或尷尬場面時，老外也會自嘲或辯解一下：

例如：

Sorry, I am late; I really need to allow myself more time next time.

抱歉，我遲到了；我下次應該給自己更充分的時間。

Gracious, I seem to be having a hard time today. Maybe I am out of step.

啊呀，我今天似乎很不對勁，也許什麼都做不好。

(gracious＝my goodness; out of step＝not doing my job well)

I just forgot to finish it; I need to make sure I remember next time.

我只是忘了把它做完；我下回一定要記得。

I really blew it, Sir. I am blowing (或 have blown) it big time. I'll make sure I don't blow it again.

先生，我真正做錯了；我大錯特錯，我要確保下回不要再錯。

(to blow it＝to make a mistake; to blow it big time＝to make a big mistake)
(可用動詞任何時態)

This morning I have already had three strikes against me.

今早我真是困難重重。

(three strikes 本指棒球賽，意思是 difficult time 或 I am out.；如果是 two strikes 是指再一球就輸了，意思是很危險，almost fail)

I may be out of line; I nearly died from embarrassment.

我可能說了一些不得體的話；我幾乎尷尬得要死。

(out of line＝say something inappropriate)

I can't believe I did that. I need a pie-in-the-face.(＝Someone should throw a pie on me.)

我不敢相信我會做出那樣的事，我臉上應該要被丟個派。

(老外開玩笑時，把蛋糕或派丟在臉上，表示一種輕微的處罰)

Sorry, I forgot. It just went in one ear and out the other.

抱歉，我忘了。我當時沒注意聽，左耳進右耳出。

(也就是：I was not listening.)

You finally caught me, didn't you?

你終於抓到我的把柄，不是嗎？

Well, I goofed; you got me there; I feel bad about it.

噢，我搞糟了；你糾到我的錯，我覺得不好意思。

(you got me there＝you caught my mistake.)

Ten whacks with a wet noodle for me! I'm really off base.

我要用濕麵條重打十下；我實在弄錯了。

(whack＝hit；用濕麵條打，是不會痛，故指輕微處分)(off base 本指棒球賽中不在壘上＝wrong direction；也有人用 way off base 更加強調)

Yes, I remember that; I just didn't get around to it.

是的，我記得；我只不過是沒有時間去做而己。

（didn't get around to it＝didn't have the time to do it.）

You can say that again! I have got trouble in spades.

你對了，我肯定麻煩來了。

（in spades＝definitely or really or a lot）（You can say that again!＝You are right. ＝I agree with you.）

I am playing the devil's advocate and I hope you don't mind.

我在跟你唱反調，希望你不介意。

（devil's advocate，字面意思是魔鬼的使者、代言人）

I hope you don't mind what I said; I am just a person calling a spade a spade.

我希望你不介意我所說的；我是有啥說啥的人。

（to call a spade a spade 字面意思是看到撲克牌拿黑桃牌，就說是黑桃，表示老老實實，＝truthfully）

I know why you have turned down my request. At least I tried and next time maybe I will succeed.

我知道你為什麼拒絕我的要求，至少我嘗試過，說不定下回我能成功！

I do things not just because someone else may be doing it.

我做事，不是因為別人做了我才做。

The boundaries I am setting for myself seem reasonable.

我為自己設定的界限似乎很合理。

為個人談吐而辯解：

I always get rattled in the presence of beautiful women.

我在美女面前，常常緊張而不自在。(因緊張而話說不好)

（get rattled＝get nervous）

I speak loudly enough to make certain that people hear what I say.

我說話聲音大，是要確定某些人聽見我所說的。

I make a special effort to speak clearly by not running my words together.

我盡量想法說得清楚，以免咬字不清。

I'm not sure if I made my answer clear. I may have confused you.

我不知道我的回答是否清楚，也許我讓你糊塗了。

A short speech may not be the best speech, but the best speech is a short one.

簡短的演講，未必是最好的演講，但最好的演講，卻是簡短的。

Chinese and English are very different languages to learn. I know my English is a little rusty.

學習中、英文有很大區別。我知道我的英語還很生疏。

（rusty 指過去學過，但很久不用而「生鏽」了）

One is never too old to learn another language. I hope I can improve my English.

一個人絕不會太老而不能學習另一個語言。我希望我能改進我的英文。

為個子矮而辯解：

Certainly. I am a shorty / shortie, but people should be measured from their eye-brows up, not from top to bottom. It's not how big or tall you are; it's how much you know.

的確，我是位小個兒，不過量人高矮，該從他們的眉毛往上量，而不是從頭往腳量。也不是看你多大或多高，而是看你的知識有多少。

或說：

Good things like diamonds come in small packages. Many great people are not tall in stature.

鑽石那樣好東西，都是放在小盒裡。許多大人物也都不是大個子。

或說：

It's not the size of the dog in the fight, but the size of the fight in the dog.

狗和狗打鬥，不是看狗的大小，而是看狗多敢鬥。

也就是：It is how brave the dog is. 或：It is not by size that you win or fail.

為某些偏見而辯解：

America is a diverse country; speaking English with an accent makes a person unique and special.

美國是個多元化的國家，一個人說英語有口音，更顯得獨特。

We are different only because your ancestor came here before mine did.

我們的不同只在你的祖先來這裡，比我的祖先早。

Patriotism is to remember the principles America was built on. It is not trying to infringe on the rights of people who are not exactly the same as you.

愛國主義是要記得美國立國的原則，而不是侵犯那些與你不盡相同人的權利。

People respect one another for who they are, not for what we would like them to be.

人們彼此尊重，是因為他們原來是怎麼樣的人，而不是因為我們要他們成為怎樣的人。

　　註：老外的婉拒或解窘，都很簡單明瞭，即使解釋理由，也是抓住重點，絕不囉嗦。

　　老美比較「能上能下」，對面子問題，一般不太重視。遇到出醜，多半也是一笑了之。這點，許多老中可以借鏡。

Chapter 8

老美情緒起伏
的說法

　　美國人情緒不好時，也時常用些口語，或含蓄的字眼，說出原味十足的英語。

　　下面這些例句，都是日常生活中常用的，有時與老外朋友「交流」時，也許可以「賣弄」一番。（例句多用第三人稱，使用時，視情況需要，可改變人稱、動詞時態或單複文）這裡分兩方面來說：

鬧情緒（Gtting upset）

She is not in the mood for talking to him about this topic.

她情緒不好，不想與他談論這個話題。

（to be in the mood 心情舒暢）

He noticed a bitter edge creeping into her tone.

他注意到她的口氣中，慢慢帶著刻薄的味道。

（bitter 有苦味，怨恨的；edge 是邊緣，銳利；creep 本是爬行，這裡是慢慢出現）

She is out of line with her feelings.

她的心情有些反常。

（to be out of line 舉止不當或不近情理＝unreasonable）

He has been brutalized and belittled by her cutting remarks.

她的刺心話語，使他受到嚴厲的指責和貶低。

（brutalize 殘酷地待人，也就是 verbally bitten；belittle 是小看或貶低；cutting remarks 與 bitter edge 意思相似）

Having a little tiff, they badmouthed each other.

他們有個小爭執，彼此謾罵。

（tiff 是小口角＝minor argument；badmouth 是說壞話）

His habit of shouting annoys me no end.

他大聲喊叫的習慣，讓我十分厭煩。

（no end 是無限，非常＝extremely）

What he said really got under her skin.

他所說的，實在令她生氣。

（to get under someone's skin 令人生氣）

He doesn't know why she has been resentful and cranky all day.

他不曉得為何她整天都很憤怒和暴躁。

（resentful 是忿忿不平，充滿怨氣；cranky 是脾氣不好＝moody or irritated）

When she speaks of him, she calls him names and uses foul language.

她一談到他就罵他，並且用些粗話。

（to call someone names 辱罵某人＝name-calling；foul 本是惡臭、骯髒的；這裡＝inappropriate）

Should he confront her about this issue or let it slide?

關於這件事，他應該與她對抗，還是隨它去算了？

(slide 本是滑落，悄悄地走；動詞時態是 slid, slid; let it slide＝let it go)

He made no attempt to hide his ill-feelings toward her.

他不想隱瞞對她的猜忌。

(to make no attempt 沒有企圖；ill-feeling 敵意、猜忌)

He simply has a chip on his shoulder toward others.

他簡直對其他人都懷有敵意。

(a chip on one's shoulder＝tendency to get mad)

Lying is her pet peeve, particularly when her boyfriend does.

說謊是她最討厭的事，尤其是她的男友說謊。

(pet 這裡是格外的或特別的；peeve 是惱怒；所以 pet peeve 是指經常抱怨或令人煩惱的事)

If he hears another complaint, he will blow his top.

假如他再聽到埋怨，他會氣得發瘋。

(to blow one's top 是非常激動，大發脾氣)

She almost lost her cool when he asked her in all seriousness.

當他問她那些嚴肅性的細節時，她近乎生氣了。

(嚴肅性的細節，包括侵犯隱私權等)(intrusive or private questions)(to lose one's cool＝almost get mad; in all seriousness 當副詞片語，修飾 asked，＝seriously)

She has a falling-out with him; I don't see what all the fuss was about.

她與他的關係緊繃，但我看不出有什麼大不了的事。

(to fall out with someone＝to strain relationship with someone；falling-out 當名詞；fuss 指沒有意義的爭吵＝pointless argument)

He goes out of his way to be rude and does things out of pure spite.

他盡量顯示粗魯，做些令人不悅的事。

(out of one's way 盡力＝make extra effort；out of pure spite＝out of nastiness；spite 本是惡意)

Mr. A works for a clod who rides herd on him all the time.

A 先生為一位不懂禮貌的人工作，常常讓他惱火。

(clod 指舉止粗魯的人＝ill-mannered person；to ride herd on someone 讓人厭煩＝to make someone irritate)

He is about to foam at the mouth upon learning his wife's cheating on him.

他知道太太欺騙他後，非常生氣。

(foam 指發怒時唾沫四濺＝froth；to foam at the mouth＝very angry)

Being very picky, he always starts in on his wife.

他很挑剔，常找他太太的毛病。

(to start in on someone 找某人的毛病＝to find fault with someone 或 to pick on someone)

After a heated discussion with her hubby, she yelled and stormed off.

她與老公激烈辯論後，咆哮起來，氣呼呼地離開。

(to storm off＝to storm out，也就是 to walk away with anger)

Having an on-again and off-again relationship with her, he has beaten her up on several occasions.

他與她關係，是斷斷續續的，他有幾次還揍她一頓。

(on-again and off-again 當形容詞用，即時有時無，與 on and off 意義相似；to beat someone up 痛打某人)

Never in a million years would I have thought he was an abusive husband.

我萬萬沒想到他竟然是位虐待妻子的人。

He seemed always at his wit's end and sometimes lost his temper big time.

他似乎常常束手無策，有時大發脾氣。

(at one's wit's / wits' end 是指令人困擾，不知所措；big time 在這裡＝very much)

Her husband's wrong-doing curled her hair.

她老公的惡行，使她極度惱火。

(to curl someone's hair 惹惱某人)

She nearly hit the ceiling when you told her about her husband's poor behavior.

當你告訴她有關她老公的不良行為時，她氣得近乎發瘋。

（to hit the ceiling 勃然大怒＝really angry）

Mr. B got so worked up and judgmental.

B 先生是如此的激動和固執己見。

（to get so worked up 如此激動；judgmental 固執己見＝opinionated）

He blew up at her when she accused him of being a pervert.

當她指控他是性變態者，他氣炸了。

（to blow up at someone 向某人大發脾氣＝extremely mad；pervert 多指性反常者，也就是 sex abuser）

His nose was completely out of joint and he hung up on her.

他心煩意亂，氣得掛斷她的電話。

（one's nose is out of joint 很厭煩＝upset；to hang up on someone 生氣而掛斷了某人的電話）（動詞時態；hang, hung, hung）

He was extremely upset and chewed her out, to say the least.

至少可以說，他是太惱火了，狠狠地罵她一頓。

（to chew someone out 嚴厲的責罵＝to scold someone severely；to say the least ＝the best way I can put it）

The last straw came when her boss spoke to her with demeaning and suggestive comments.

當她的老闆向她說些低級和調情的話時，她已忍無可忍。

（the last straw＝the straw that broke the camel's back 即一連串不愉快的事而令人最後無法忍受；demean 是有辱人格）

Because of his intimidation, she was really teed off.

由於他的威脅，她真的發火了。

(動詞 intimidate 是恐嚇或威脅；動詞 tee 本是高爾夫開球，但 to tee off 是生氣或發怒＝to tick off)

His constantly rude manners have driven her up the wall.

他粗魯的行為，使她非常憤怒。

(to drive someone up the wall 令某人十分惱火＝to get on someone's nerves)

She is steamed enough to stop seeing him again.

她氣夠了，不再理他。

(steam 動詞是發出蒸氣，名詞是水蒸氣；to be steamed 是生氣或發怒＝to get steamed)

His inconsideration has left her hot under the collar.

他不為別人著想的作風，使她生氣。

(inconsiderate 是形容詞，不體諒別人；hot under the collar 照字義是衣領下會發熱，也就是很惱火，生氣)

He certainly will see red should you start criticizing his work.

假如你開始批評他的工作，他一定會冒火。

(to see red 是火冒三丈；也可以說：He really saw red when his plans broke down.但通常不用：He is seeing red 或 He has seen red 等時態，只用 get angry 代替)

Here is little agreement and a lot of argument between them.

他們之間很少意見一致，都是爭吵不休。

As a nag, he cusses and puts his wife down quite often.

他是愛找別人毛病的人,經常罵太座,貶低她。

(nag 喜歡指責抱怨者,也當動詞,時態是:nagged, nagging;cuss 是咒罵,curse 的變體字;to put someone down 把某人貶低,小看某人;put-down 也當名詞用,如:He hurts her with his put-downs.)

He seems to have an ax to grind with any individual.

他似乎與任何人都有觀點上爭吵的理由。

(to have an ax to grind 為某種觀點不同而爭吵)

She was appalled by his rude behavior; her tolerance slipped closer to the boiling point.

他的粗魯行為使她驚訝,她的容忍將至臨界點。

(appall＝appeal 使驚駭,動詞時態;appalled, appalling＝surprised or shocked;to slip closer 逐漸進入＝nearly has reached;boiling point 沸點)

His pressure and frustration have built to the breaking point; he yells and screams but not get physical.

他的壓力和挫折感已達到極限;他大聲喊叫,但沒粗野動手。

(breaking point 指爆發點與 boiling point 意思相似;to get physical 指動手毆打)

He likes to rock the boat and to get into a hassle.

他喜歡製造麻煩,發生衝突。

(rock 本是岩石,這裡是動詞,指劇烈震動;to rock the boat 是搗亂＝to make trouble;hassle 是爭吵或衝突)

He held a grudge and refused to speak to any of the group.

他為過去的事懷恨在心，不跟那些人說話。

(grudge 是積怨＝revengeful or resentful for past offense；to hold a grudge against someone 為過去錯誤對某人懷恨在心；也可用 to have 或 to bear a grudge)

He attempts to even the score by fighting fire with fire.

他企圖進行報復，以牙還牙。

(to even the score 本是拉平，也就是進行報復＝to get even；to fight fire with fire 以火攻火＝to do the same as others do to you)

Shouting and foot-stomping with surly speech have become his personality.

大喊大叫、跳腳和粗魯言語，成為他的個性。

(foot-stomping 是名詞，指跺腳，不用 feet-stomping；如果說：when he got mad, he stomped his feet，則不用 foot；surly 是粗魯的＝rude)

As he threw such a fit, they ended up in a fight.

因為他大發脾氣，他們最後打起架來。

(to throw a fit / fits 大為發怒＝to have a fit)

較冷靜（**Calming down**）

When you feel you are about to blow your stack, go outside for a few minutes.

你要生氣時，出去走幾分鐘。

（to blow one's stack 發脾氣，勃然大怒＝to blow one's top 或 lid）

He may help her to let go of her anger.

他也許能幫她消除憤怒。

（to let go of something 放開或不追究或付諸一笑）

He should cool down and not drop the bomb.

他應該冷靜下來，不要讓情況惡化。

（to drop the bomb＝to make situation worse）

If he keeps this matter impersonal, everything will be hunky dory.

假如他不讓這件事受個人感情的影響，那麼一切都會平安無事。

（hunky dory 是讓人滿意的，頂呱呱的）

Try to keep your nose out of his business.

盡量不要管他的閒事。

（to keep one's nose out of someone's business 別管別人的事）

Don't fight fire with fire because it might create a bigger fire.

不要以火攻火，因為那會造成更大的火。

No hassles; try not to fly off the handle.

不要爭吵；盡量別發脾氣。

(hassle 是爭吵＝argument；to fly off the handle＝to lose temper)

They should not start demanding an eye for an eye and a tooth for a tooth in this matter.

他們對這件事，不要作以眼還眼，以牙還牙的要求。

(an eye for an eye 就是採取同樣的手段回擊。與 a tooth for a tooth 意思相似 ＝take even revenge)

Over this touchy topic, he wants to stay above the fray.

關於這個敏感的話題，他要避免衝突。

(fray 本是吵架或衝突；to stay above the fray＝to avoid conflict)

Count to ten slowly; once you have calmed down, you will be better able to act in a rational manner.

慢慢地從一數到十，一旦冷靜下來，你就更能用理智的方式處理。

(rational manner＝normal manner)

Try to make an effort to mend fences; don't be a narrow-minded snob.

設法修補彼此的關係，不要成為一位心胸狹窄自命不凡者。

(注意：sonb 是個自負傲慢者；slob 是衣冠不整，舉止粗魯者)

Stop beating yourself up over such trivia.

不要為這小事，太責難自己。

(to beat oneself up 與自己過不去，責難自己；trivia 是拉丁文，是芝麻小事＝trivial thing)

You will get nowhere if you take a hard-line stance all the time.

如果你一直採取強硬的立場，你就無法取得進展。

(to get nowhere 毫無進展，徒勞無功；hard-line stance 不妥協立場＝hard-line position)

He needs to respect her advice to turn the other cheek in order not to lay an egg on this issue.

他需要尊重她的勸告，寬恕別人，才不致搞砸這件事。

(to turn the other cheek 是挨轟後，把另一面頰湊上，也就是甘受侮辱或寬恕別人＝forgive；to lay an egg on something 把某件事搞砸了＝to mess up something)

Sorry to hurt your feelings; I did not mean to get personal.

抱歉傷了你的感情，我不是要涉入人身攻擊的。

(to get personal 涉入隱私或人身攻擊)

They seem to be at cross purposes; they should forget the whole thing.

他們似乎彼此誤會；他們應該忘掉整件事。

(at cross purposes 相互矛盾，彼此誤解)

Please forgive any inadvertent pain it caused you.

請原諒由於疏忽而造成你的痛苦。

(inadvertent 是粗心大意，疏忽無意＝unintentional；名詞是 inadvertence)

Don't let this matter get your goat.

不要讓這件事使你惱火。

(to get someone's goat＝to bother or upset someone 使某人發怒)

I really feel bad because I blew it big time.

我真是感到抱歉，因為我犯了一次大錯。(it 可指某件事)

(to blow it big time 弄得一團糟或犯錯＝to make a mistake；動詞時態：blow, blew, blown)

Do not find yourself trapped in a web of finger-pointing, criticism, and fault-finding when there is a problem.

有問題時，不要把你自己陷入指責、批評和挑剔的圈裡。

(web 是糾纏或圈套；to point the finger at 是指責，finger-pointing 當名詞；to find fault with someone 找別人的錯誤，trap 是陷入困境，fault-finding 當名詞；to find yourself trapped＝to trap yourself)

If he is uptight about every little thing, he will have a horrible time.

如果他對每件小事都容易發怒，那他就糟透了。

A quick temper does not bring success.

容易發脾氣的個性，不會帶來成功。

(quick temper＝short fuse)

For this situation, he wishes they all might have 20-20 foresight in solving the problem.

在此情形，他盼望他們能有最好的遠見，解決問題。

（foresight 是預見或有先見之明；20-20 foresight 本是最好的視力，也就是 perfect vision or prediction）

Swallow your anger / pride and try to make a friend of him.

忍住你的怒火／傲氣，設法與他做朋友。

（swallow 本是嚥下或抑制；to swallow one's anger 克制憤怒）

Anger is like casting a stone into a wasp's nest.

發怒就像對著蜂窩拋投石頭一樣。（會被蜂螫）

（wasp 是黃蜂；cast 是拋投；動詞過去式及過去分詞都是 cast）

Now he may have a choice between eating humble pie or（eating）crow.

現在他只有一個承認錯誤的選擇。

（to eat humble pie 和 to eat crow 意思相似，都是被迫承認錯誤）

High emotions may cause people to say regrettable things.

情緒激動時，會說出令人遺憾的事。

Try to keep the lid on your emotion at work.

工作時，盡量控制自己的情緒。

（to keep the lid on something 抑住或隱瞞某事）

As he didn't mean what he said to her, she will forgive his speaking out of turn.

他對她所說的，不是那個意思，她會原諒他不該說的話。

(to speak out of turn 說不該說的話＝said something he should not have)

It is not worth letting the situation rattle you.

這情況讓你惱火，是不值得的。

(rattle 本是碰撞作聲，這裡是煩惱或生氣)

Trying to handle bickering people requires some personal skills.

處理愛爭吵的人，需要一些人際的技巧。

(bicker 是喜歡爭吵的＝argumentative)

No one should raise a hand in anger toward others.

任何人生氣時，都不可動手打人。

They need to grow up enough to forgive and forget.

他們應該做足夠成熟的人，寬恕別人，忘掉舊惡。

(forgive and forget 是句口語，就是不念舊惡)

It is said that the greatest remedy for anger is delay.

據說生氣最大的療法就是拖延。

Linking English
如何和老外打交道：基本英語禮儀、推薦、情緒表達法

2011年12月初版　　　　　　　　　　　　　　　定價：新臺幣290元
有著作權・翻印必究
Printed in Taiwan.

著　　　者　懷　　　　　中	
發 行 人　林　載　爵	

出　版　者	聯 經 出 版 事 業 股 份 有 限 公 司	叢書編輯　李　　　　　芃
地　　　址	台 北 市 基 隆 路 一 段 1 8 0 號 4 樓	校　　對　王　沂　璇
編 輯 部 地 址	台 北 市 基 隆 路 一 段 1 8 0 號 4 樓	內文排版　陳　如　琪
叢書主編電話	（ 0 2 ） 8 7 8 7 6 2 4 2 轉 2 2 6	封面設計　Lilly Lai
台北聯經書房	台 北 市 新 生 南 路 三 段 9 4 號	
電　　　話	（ 0 2 ） 2 3 6 2 0 3 0 8	
台 中 分 公 司	台 中 市 健 行 路 3 2 1 號	
暨 門 市 電 話	（ 0 4 ） 2 2 3 7 1 2 3 4 e x t . 5	
郵 政 劃 撥 帳 戶	第 0 1 0 0 5 5 9 - 3 號	
郵 撥 電 話	（ 0 2 ） 2 3 6 2 0 3 0 8	
印　刷　者	文 聯 彩 色 製 版 印 刷 有 限 公 司	
總　經　銷	聯 合 發 行 股 份 有 限 公 司	
發　行　所	台北縣新店市寶橋路235巷6弄6號2樓	
電　　　話	（ 0 2 ） 2 9 1 7 8 0 2 2	

行政院新聞局出版事業登記證局版臺業字第0130號

本書如有缺頁，破損，倒裝請寄回聯經忠孝門市更換。　ISBN　978-957-08-3938-8 (平裝)
聯經網址：www.linkingbooks.com.tw
電子信箱：linking@udngroup.com

國家圖書館出版品預行編目資料

如何和老外打交道：基本英語禮
儀、推薦、情緒表達法/懷中著．初版．
臺北市．聯經．2011年12月（民100年）．
272面．14.8×21公分（Linking English）
ISBN　978-957-08-3938-8（平裝）

1.英語　2.讀本

805.18　　　　　　　　　　100024846